one *if*

A VIRAGO FANTASY

CAROL B. ALLEN

M

Metropolitan Publishing

Metropolitan Publishing, New York
2019

ISBN: 978-1-7343424-0-6
Library of Congress Control Number: 1-73434-240-4

First Edition
Printed in the United States of America

For
Skylar, Sloane, Austin, and Tyler
Always believe in yourself and the possibilities
inspired by your dreams.

chapter one

Parker pressed her nose to the frosty glass. Her eyes stared down the frisky hummingbird darting about her terrace then drifted back to her laptop and the experiment she was scheduled to present at school in the morning. It was the magic hour, just before dusk. The lampposts glowed as Central Park readied to settle into the hush of a quiet snowy evening ahead.

Outside, the daring bird torpedoed toward her face, rammed into the glass, then dashed away. Over the past several weeks, the same bird had been performing drop-ins, incessantly rapping at her window and disrupting her studies after school. Of all the windows in all the buildings across the city, how had the hummingbird found hers over and over again? And in the dead of winter! What did it want from her anyway?

Today she'd had enough. Her inquisitive nature won. She grinned at the bird, crinkled her nose, knit her brows, and sent the corners of her mouth into their quizzical pattern. Could she get the bird to come to her? Parker grabbed a jacket, opened the terrace door, and stepped outside. A light wind tousled her long, wavy brown hair and billowed the hem of her pleated skirt. Despite the cold, the fresh air felt good. So pretty tonight, she thought.

Tiptoeing through the icy snowflakes, she approached the bird slowly, opened her arms and motioned to the hummingbird to come toward her. The bird's white-tipped tail feathers fluttered away and its dainty twig-like feet, frail as matchsticks, grazed the top of the wrought iron terrace balustrade. Parker edged closer. Her fingers whitened as she clung to the metal. Her mind galloped forward and her eyes swept downward along the rows of bay windows and their respective cornices, all eighteen stories of them, to the traffic plodding along Central Park West.

Parker lightened her hold and faced the hummingbird's distinctive black triangular marking centered above its beak—right smack in the middle of its head. She leaned over the handrail, her tummy balancing on the slippery metal. The bird dangled before her in the air. She extended her hand to the bird.

Just as her heart skipped a beat, Parker lost her footing, stumbled, and toppled over the rail.

She plunged downward. Consumed by panic, she grabbed for something, anything, but she plummeted headfirst, out of control toward the pavement, and the terrifying thought of hitting it...

Blackness devoured her. Pulled by an odd magnetic force, Parker was drawn into a dark, jelly-like tube. She fell faster, accelerating, bouncing along the curving path of gel, waves of nausea and dizziness surging inside her belly. The unending, sloshing movement slowed.

The impact she expected never came. She was alive.

chapter two

From above, white-hot light hammered her head. Parker closed her eyes. Where was she? In a hospital? Had she slipped and landed back on the terrace? Lying down, she ran her hands over her bare arms, wiping away the perspiration coating her body like a suffocating blanket she couldn't throw off. She lifted each foot to make sure her legs were functioning. Nothing hurt. At least she hadn't broken any bones. Then, her fingers touched her shoulder. A strange textured material had replaced her Tate Academy school uniform and covered her—from her torso down to her ankles. Could she be wearing a hospital gown?

From a distance, she heard what sounded like bird calls. An orchestra of chirping in brash, cackling tones. The sounds grew louder. She blinked and the stark whiteness infiltrated the slits of her narrowed lids. She briefly glimpsed jagged, white fluffy pillows of clouds in all shapes and sizes. No land in evidence anywhere she could see, just a blue reflective kind of watery surface a far distance below her. She floated on a rocking sea of air, shifting ever so slightly, rising slightly up, and lowering back down. Could she be in heaven?

Then the brightness beating on her and the strangeness of the sights forced her to shut her eyes tight. For good measure, she ground her palms into her eyelids, and rubbed around to make sure they weren't malfunctioning.

Someone approached and touched her shoulder. "Mom, are you here? Dad?" she called, praying for an answer.

"Parker." A kind, grandfatherly voice said, "Ahhh, you are safe." The voice sounded hollow and far away as if projected from within an echo chamber. Parker clutched the odd fabric covering her, pulled her knees to her chest, and hugged herself for protection. "Are you my doctor? Am I okay? Where are my parents?" Her breath rasped in and out.

"You needn't be afraid, Parker." The voice's owner knew her name. "You are in the Upperworld, on Spyridon."

Spyridon was not a hospital in New York! His words toppled out like jumbled letters on a Scrabble board. She struggled to process every word.

"I am Stefanos, the Sky King, the Ruling Great One of the Upperworld. I am glad you arrived safely. It is not an easy journey from Earth." His tone felt warm and endearing, and still approached from what seemed a long, echoing hall, though a bit closer now.

She couldn't avoid it any longer. Parker struggled for

air and pushed herself to sit up. The movement reminded her of floating as if sitting up midair. Parker told herself to work through these challenges one step at a time. First, the speaker.

She forced her eyes to squint in the direction of the voice. An ancient face covered in ashen feathers, absent of color, stared back at her. Parker concentrated on the bird-like features, mostly the eyes, too nervous to note much beyond the imposing, massive head. Deep crevices tracked along the feathery skin. Black-brown eyes, set deeply in a peaked forehead, penetrated hers. The prominent beak-like nose thrust forth like a mountain between two glimmering pools for eyes. The words sprung from his beak. He looked like an eagle, yet something about him seemed human! Her eyes traveled in amazement along the length of the colossal being crouched beside her. His head had to measure the size of her own nearly six-foot frame.

The infinite sea stretching out far below her, in literally every direction, merged with the distant sky. Hard to discern the horizon. Only the gently lapping waves some distance below gave her an idea of her place in the sky.

She wondered if she were dead and choked on the horrifying thought. Her voice deserted her as she hunted for words.

"No, I assure you—you are very much alive."

He saw what she was thinking! No one had ever read her mind before. Sometimes her parents might figure out her thoughts, but they could. They knew her.

"Spyr-- you said Spyridon?"

"Yes. Another world."

"What about my parents? What will they think is going on? Um, do they know where I am?"

"Spyridon shares the same galaxy as Earth. But time travels differently here than on your planet. When you go home, it will be as if you never left. Your family, and those on Earth, well, they do not even know you are gone."

Parker tried to absorb his words. Could it be possible her parents wouldn't know what happened to her? Her body shook uncontrollably, and she gasped when she saw that she wore a rough textured, white linen sheath.

"What is this I am wearing? What happened to my clothes?" She pulled her knees to her chest again and tried not to think about how her clothes had been changed.

"You wear the dress of the Upperworld. You'll be more comfortable in our climate. It's quite warm here."

The eagle rustled his voluminous cape, jostling with his every movement. She glimpsed gray quills peeking out from the edge of the fabric. Wings, she wondered. Nauseous and faint, Parker struggled with the knowledge of being airborne and the feeling of standing on trembling, shaky feet. The air was so thin, her head began to spin, and her chest grew tight.

"It takes a bit to get used to—our atmosphere and the elevation." The old eagle moved a talon-hand to a worn bronze medallion suspended from a braided vine circling his neck.

"We're flying!"

Stefanos chuckled. "My kind are always flying. The

Spirits lift you. I hope the disorientation passes soon. We have a great deal of work to do."

He fingered the metal and placed the talon-finger on hers and gazed into her eyes.

Parker wanted to hide from his stare. If she had ever doubted whether she had a soul, now didn't qualify as one of those moments. Her insides exposed, this creature, this eagle-like thing, knew her inner being. She had never felt so naked.

He murmured, "You are here to help our people. More earthlings will be joining us shortly. I will explain everything when they arrive. After you've had some rest. Come."

With another touch of the medallion he wore, Parker began to feel the rush of the wind as she rose through the air at great speed. She sucked in several deep, terrified breaths, wondering if she would be taking off into space before she caught sight of him a few feet ahead of her, to her right. They leveled off and sped up even further. Flying like this went on for long enough and she began to enjoy the sensation, despite the beating sun and the feeling she wasn't getting enough air with each breath. A great structure appeared, first as a dot, but it quickly resolved into a huge floating elaborate mansion or maybe even a castle.

Before she could get a better look, she rushed towards the structure, and then over it. She swooped down at alarming speed into the side of the thing. A gigantic glass window slid aside for her, and she skidded and stumbled to a stop.

"I will leave you here. Answers will come soon, as well

as my spirit guide, Belliza. You will recognize her. For now, Parker, I say goodbye, and it has been my pleasure to meet you."

The creature rose to its full height, and Parker took in his physical presence, astounded by the enormity of his sheer size, several feet taller than she. The old eagle lifted himself up from the ground with ease, barely stirring the air around him. He rose further without a backward glance. She tracked his ascent until he became a mere disappearing speck. Alone again, she wished he'd stayed. So many questions remained.

chapter three

Thousands of puffy clouds both large and small circled the white windowed room in a carousel of movement. Parker's eyes stayed glued to the glass. A blanket of blue sky belched rotating cloud puffs in baffling formations. Clouds whirled past her shaped like buildings, animals, bridges, a lone horse's skull, clusters of tiny fish, even a basket of apples. Most of the clouds were pierced by indistinguishable, barren tree limbs, twisted and dead-looking in weather-worn gray. Like a lab rat in a perseverance experiment, Parker had been sequestered in the glass-enclosed space without a means of measuring how much time had elapsed. The blazing sun hadn't moved any noticeable distance and heated the room to a stifling hot temperature.

The glass wall opened, and two teenagers tumbled toward her like rolling dice. Parker dodged the spinning bodies as they looped in the air, barely missing her before they bounced on the cushiony floor as if on a trampoline.

She thought back to the old eagle's words. More

earthlings would be coming. Oddly, she felt relieved. At least, she wouldn't be alone. Did the hummingbird hoodwink them, too? Had they met the old eagle?

Her eyes jockeyed back and forth between the boy and the girl. They seemed about her age and returned her gaze with blank, dazed expressions. They wore the same weird sacks as Parker's. She'd spent some time inspecting hers, and the best she could tell, it was woven in some kind of light plant fiber.

Parker's heart pounded in her chest, and her head throbbed. Always shy and uneasy with the kids at school, she had never been comfortable around the other students. The only ones who befriended her were classmates who pretended to like her to get the answers for AP Bio. Parker had already aced the course a year early and had moved on to AP Environmental Studies.

Parker tried to calm herself and turned her attention to the boy. He'd failed to even glance at her or the girl since entering the room. Big and barrel-chested, he stood around six feet eight or nine. He could have been one of those football types all the girls gushed about. Parker nearly chuckled to herself visualizing him playing football while dressed in the bizarre get-up. For once, her height felt normal, almost petite.

He had smooth ebony skin and a full head of thick, curly hair, growing freely in every direction. One of the boys at her high school had the same fun hair. The girl was stunning, tiny and graceful with silken black hair and porcelain ivory skin. A light fringe of bangs dusted her forehead. Her earlier blank daze had morphed to an angry red. Parker feared giving her a second glance, let alone attempting to talk to her, figuring the girl could explode.

Parker fought back her insecurity. She couldn't blow up these relationships and walk away like at home. None of them wanted to be there. She needed them. They needed each other. She gathered her courage and tried to break through. "I don't know who you are. And, I'm guessing neither of you knows anything about me. But I think this is real. Our brains aren't making any of this up."

They listened, but neither responded.

Clenching her jaw, she pressed ahead. "My name's Parker." She paused and fumbled on, "The last thing I remember I'm in my bedroom after school and this hummingbird is outside my room, tapping its beak on the glass and making me nuts. At first, I'm thinking it's pretty bizarre a bird up this high. And even weirder, the bird's knocking its beak nonstop into my window. Finally, I can't take it anymore and I open the door, and before I know what is happening, I'm in this long, dark tube and I end up here." She decided not to reveal she thought the bird wanted to teach her to fly.

The girl ignored her and ran to the windows and banged her fists against the glass. Even if she had managed to break the glass, where would that put her? In a cloudy pillow with protruding sticks?

"Uh, I met a…well uh, his name is Stefanos, and he said he needed us to help. He told me we're in a place called Spyridon." Parker studied them. If they trusted their senses, they'd come to recognize the truth quickly. Beneath the teasing and the attempt to use her to cheat, Parker knew people as rational beings. Some just needed more time than others to get past their emotions.

The girl spun around, her black hair swinging in sync like a model in a television ad promoting shampoo for gorgeous, perfect hair. Her face, however, contorted into a mask of rage.

"Shut your mouth," Henley snapped.

"I'm only trying to help," Parker said. "Listen, if we--"

The girl lunged at Parker, and with nostrils flaring, she shoved Parker hard, shaking the trim on Parker's sheath, flinging some of the golden feathers into the air. Parker tripped, caught her balance, and glared back at the girl.

"What if we never get out of this place?" The girl screamed, "We don't know what they want from us. And you don't either. Don't be an idiot."

Parker back-stepped to put some distance between them. She began pacing, orbiting the glass space and using her nervous energy to unravel the mystery of where they might be and how to deal with her two new companions. She spoke out loud, though for her own reassurance. She noted the vastness of the room's perimeter, the depth and height of the walls, busying her mind and praying a clue on how she could communicate with them would come to her. Peering through the glass into the distance, she wondered if life existed on Spyridon. Human? Living, breathing somethings? If nothing else, had the hummingbird been watching them?

"Chill out," Parker snapped at the girl, suddenly embarrassed by her own harsh words so unlike her timid nature. She had never spoken to anyone like that before, but she couldn't let the girl walk all over her.

The boy had moved to the window, his eyes fixed straight ahead. He turned back around and said to Parker, "I'm Edison. From Detroit." Grateful for the response, she guessed he wanted to break the tension. He leaned against the glass, crossed his arms and said, "And where are we anyway? What's Spyridon? Do either of you have a clue?" He spoke softly, nodding his head, the curls moving with him as he lowered his gaze to the floor. Parker admired his composure.

Parker answered, "I only know what I've been told— if talking birds count!" Oops. The words spilled out before she could catch them. Maybe they hadn't met up with the hummingbird. Neither had mentioned it and now they would think she was certifiably crazy!

The girl laughed derisively. "Talks to birds! This idiot talks to birds. I bet you are friends with that annoying hummingbird!"

She confirmed Parker's suspicion: she definitely had seen the little bird.

"We have no weapons. No anything—not that any of us would know what to do with them anyway. How are we even going to survive? In the clouds? Eating worms? I don't know what's going on, and I don't know about you two, but I have a life in California, and I'm not playing their stupid game."

Parker wondered if the girl's cold stare and tough talk were real because her own dwindling courage had now disappeared. The girl snipped back, "Why should I trust you? We don't know anything about you!"

"Hey, look at her. She's one of us," Edison said. Thankfully, he kept his cool and addressed the girl. "So, you're from California. What's your name?"

"Henley," the girl said and added, "Not that it matters. I just want to go back to where I came from. There is no reason for me to be here. You know that expression 'it's for the birds'? Well, this place is for the birds! Not me!"

"Birds and humans do have a little in common, you know. Scientifically speaking, birds have big brains. Their brains are comparatively the same scale as our brains are to our bodies. I'm just saying."

"Oh my god, you're a nerd." Henley said. "Oh my god! Kill me right now. What are you some kind of walking Wikipedia? Even if you are smart, you don't know anything about this place. You and that hummingbird can kiss my--"

At that moment, Edison began to hum the sweetest and purest sound Parker ever heard. Henley's posture changed. She relaxed the stiffness in her shoulders and began chanting in a language Parker didn't understand, maybe Chinese.

Surreal. Just like everything else.

chapter four

A sweet aroma filtered into the room as one of the glass walls swept open. The smell of warm honey jogged Parker's memory to the honeysuckle flowers her mom arranged in their apartment on early summer days. The thought quickly died when the hummingbird with its black marking whooshed in and hovered before her. Parker inhaled the scent and wondered if the smell would always announce the bird's arrival.

The bird flew over to Parker's side and twisted its tiny body to face Edison and Henley. Parker raised her arm to whisk it away, not about to take sides against the boy or the girl.

The bird took little notice and lisped matter-of-factly, "Parker, Edison and Henley, we are grateful you all arrived zafely." Parker was perplexed again—how did these birds know their names?

Parker retreated to her safety mode, her MO at school. She pictured herself in the classroom, staying quiet and fading into the background, hunching over her lanky frame, concerned she might say or do something to cause herself trouble. Someone had to say something! But no one reacted.

The bird dashed up, down, and sideways in constant motion. "Our Ruling Great One, the Zky King, will be here momentarily. He will explain everything to you. He wanted to wait until everyone waz together." Parker's gaze followed the bird as it wove around the room like a racquet ball randomly bouncing off the walls. "I am Belliza, your liaizon on our planet, Zpyridon. Our planetz are clozely related, though thoze on Earth don't know we exizt. We are hidden from you, but of the zame galaxy."

Edison stopped humming.

Henley seemed to reinflate with her former anger that very moment, and she stabbed a finger toward the flitting black shape. "Cut the BS. You're talking gibberish."

Parker repeated the odd names in her head—Spyridon, Ruling Great One, Belliza—and felt pressured to speak up, an unlikely reaction for her. "We have no business here," Parker told the bird, astonished again such strong words came from within her. Even worse, she was speaking and negotiating with a bird! "If we are on another planet as you say, how do we get back to Earth? Whatever you did to get us here, reverse it and let us go home." And with a gesture of politeness she added, "Please."

"Each of you haz a part in our future."

Henley jumped to her feet. "Not me. I don't belong here. Maybe those two do," Henley scowled at Parker and Edison. "But, not me! Not a chance. You have the wrong girl!" She pointed to the bird and snapped, "I am leaving! I want out of here now. You got us here, now you return us from where we came. Make it happen." Henley's eyes were guarded, and her mouth flew open as her expression transformed from astonishment to fear.

Parker turned to see the old eagle in Henley's sightline. He had entered the room on silent wings. Parker glanced over to Edison who now stood at the window, backing away from all of them as far as he could.

The eagle towered before them and opened his wings, blocking the entire width of the room behind him. Parker thought he must have intended this to be a welcoming gesture, but she was petrified as she visually absorbed the enormity of his presence. The echoing voice of the old eagle began speaking, "I know what I am about to tell you will be difficult to understand and believe. But listen carefully, I speak the truth and you will come to learn I only speak the truth."

As Stefanos moved from the entryway, he lowered his wings and revealed another five young people standing behind him. All wore the same white sheaths along with shocked, terrified and uncomprehending expressions, identical to Parker's still tumultuous feelings. Some of them padded around the springy surface of the floor, while two immediately turned to marvel at the limitless horizon and the passing clouds.

Stefanos addressed them all, with the calm and practiced cadence of a teacher experienced in managing unruly groups. "You are safe here. I will return shortly, with more friends and more answers."

Throughout the next few hours he brought them in, by threes and fives, until nearly thirty young people crowded the glass room. Henley continued her bickering and got into two more fights. The space around her widened, yet Edison remained nearby. The muttering resumed, with plenty of guesses. Why had they been brought here? Who was the giant bird? Had everyone seen the hummingbird? From there, the cliques had formed, and Parker once again felt isolated and pushed to the outside of the groups. As always. She had answers, but the pressure of so many people stole the words from her.

When Stefanos returned, the sun still hung high in the sky, only it had swung around to the glass walls on the opposite side of the floating room.

The old eagle quietly took control of the room. "Spyridon, our planet, where you are right now, is dying. Eons ago, we were much like Earth, a world of human beings, animals, birds, insects, and fish. There is little similarity now between our planets. The path of Spyridon's environmental destruction eroded most of our land. Only one continent remains, Katamoor. You arrived in our Upperworld. It is the Upperworld which I rule. It will be clear to you we are an avian society." He stopped and Parker detected a smile forming within the edges of his beak. "Look at me. Like most Upperworlders, I am human. I speak. I think. I emote. We evolved in order to live here among the clouds in Spyridon's lower atmosphere."

The room went deadly quiet, and Parker thought how

odd for a room filled with thirty teenagers to be silent—without sound and without movement. Then, a voice called out, "Living in the clouds? That's not even possible."

After a brief stirring of muffled, contentious dialogue within the scattered groups, Henley's voice broke through and challenged the old eagle, "And how do you eat with practically no land to provide food? Or how do you breathe without oxygen? In fact, if you supposedly only speak the truth, how are we even breathing up here?"

"Only clouds and one parcel of land on an entire planet the size of Earth?" Parker couldn't help but ask. Her mind went to work, questioning everything she knew about the scientific principles behind ecosystems and sustainability and the impossibility of the eagle's claims.

The great eagle smiled kindly and pivoted his neck to take in the vision of youth throughout the room. "I applaud your discerning nature. The Spirits of the Sky ensured we would adapt to the environmental changes on our planet. They took care of us and granted us the ability to survive.

"Each of you are here because you are among the best and the brightest on Earth and I believe every one of you is uniquely suited to assist Spyridon in her hour of need. However, I will keep none of you against your will. But believe me when I say, upon your return, it will be as though no time has elapsed.

"Those of you who choose to stay, I am already in your debt. My gratitude will be endless. For those of you who wish to go, there are no hard feelings. If only my scout were able to speak to you on Earth, all could have been explained before bringing you here and upending your lives. At least for the moment.

"But now we travel to the North Gate." Once more, he touched the amulet on his feathered chest, and once more Parker felt weightlessness take hold of her. The others also lifted up off the floor, the walls slid open, and together the thirty of them soared northward.

The clouds rushed past Parker as all the teens who had been in the glass room now moved at the same dizzying pace as she did, their eyes widened in disbelief. Synchronized, they ascended above the clouds and once again she marveled at the exhilarating speed with which she moved. She practically laughed out loud, spotting the lot of them above her and below her, and thinking they traveled like a flock of birds in a v-formation, Stefanos leading the way. And, still nothing but blue sky and peculiar shaped clouds surrounded them. The sensation of wonderment thrilled her entire being.

As quickly as they rose through the sky, Stefanos stopped abruptly and swooped below to an enormous valley of cloud cover, which resembled mountain tops of varying heights. In the center loomed a black hole, a cavernous opening into the same kind of dark gelatin tube in which she traveled from Earth to Spyridon. From the noises around her, she figured most of the others recognized the portal. Stefanos stopped and gathered all of them within his wingspan.

"Welcome to the North Gate. Perhaps you are

somewhat familiar with the portal—it leads back to Earth. It is time now to make your decision. Do you stay and help us? Help us fight for our survival? And if so, no one will ever know you have been gone. Or, do you return to Earth, unharmed in any way. If you choose to return, most likely you will only remember this as a dream."

Parker's spirit sank as she watched the cliques of familiarity frame the rim of one of the cloud canyons. Small groups of three and four sought comfort with those they had bonded with upon their arrival. For them, Parker figured the nightmare neared its end. They spoke quietly amongst themselves and moved stealthily in groups toward the portal fearing they would be pulled back into the talons of the old eagle. Her belly ached with despair as one after another vanished into the black hole. She fought back her disappointment in humanity, then reminded herself that her own leap of faith could not be expected of others.

Stefanos held his beak high and had moved away to a distant peak, still within sight, but far enough removed to give them space and room to think. He was a good leader— just by observing the level of respect he showed them proved his strong moral compass. She could not desert him at this time of need, especially when she knew she would be able to help them solve their problems. Besides, the magic of Spyridon excited her. In her mind, she had already committed to stay. After all of the earthlings disappeared into the portal, only she, Edison and Henley remained.

"I am staying," Parker called out to them. "What do you think? You know we can help them." Nervously she added, "Don't you?"

Edison and Henley held their position high on the ridge opposite her. They exchanged glances. Parker thought Henley looked a bit cross. She hadn't intended to pressure her. Edison turned back to Parker and said, "I am going to stay, too. And yeah, I will help them." He took Henley's hand in his and asked, "And you? Can you handle this, Henley?"

"What makes you think I couldn't? If you're in, I'm in."

chapter five

Now they were three. Just three. But to Parker, she was on her own.

Stefanos ushered them in his wings back to the glass room. He searched their faces, his glowing eyes seeing through each of them as if peering through a magnifying glass. "I repeat myself, but I must. I am forever in your debt. Thank you."

Parker fidgeted, still questioning their roles and how they would serve to help. Edison and Henley stood apart but appeared as inquisitive as she.

"Tonight, you will be presented to our Great Ones, leaders from each of our regions in the Upperworld. This is an important evening for us. They have been apprised of your decision to stay. I assure you their gratitude will equal, if not surpass, mine. But first things first. Today, you will travel to Katamoor. My falcon escorts will arrive here in the Sky Box momentarily to guide your journey. I hope you find Katamoor as inspiring as I do. You will gain a better understanding when your eyes absorb the beauty and majesty."

The Sky Box darkened as one windowed wall dimmed to black. Six enormous gray falcons with bands of chrome yellow feathers streaking the top of their heads blocked the light from behind the huge window walls. Each easily stood as tall as she, and their silent stares gave them an air of menace. Parker shuddered and was about to ask why they needed escorts, but Henley beat her to the punch.

"Why are we going with them?"

"Well, certainly, you can't go by yourselves. You don't even know where to go," Stefanos teased. "Katamoor is a bit mystical. Maybe even magical. Besides, our Spirits live there. I wouldn't want them to think you are trespassing. When they see the falcons, they will understand your mission. I think it is important for you to survey our world and understand how we survive here before you meet our leaders tonight. It is quite a long journey, though you could go on your own, but my falcons will be the fastest way to get there and back in time." His sharp eyes blinked, "You need to return here within a few hours. The falcons are speedy and travel quickly." He laughed, "But hold on tight."

Parker tried not to question the idea of these birds of prey accompanying them. She was more comfortable with Belliza. Why would these massive falcons, really hawks, known for their formidable hunting skills, need to shepherd them? Would they be in danger on Katamoor?

Stefanos picked up her thoughts and gently said, "No harm will come to you. Your journey today is purely a tour.

Let's say for familiarity. You will be spending some time on Katamoor to solve our issues very shortly. Enjoy the beauty. I look forward to hearing your thoughts upon your return." As he spoke, the wall opened, and Parker, Henley and Edison elevated into the air and floated up towards the falcons and then each lowered into place onto the back of a falcon.

Parker held her breath and wondered if Edison or Henley knew that a falcon's flight could top two hundred miles an hour. Hold on tight? Stefanos meant—hold on for your life. Parker's long limbs clung to the falcon's boney back. She turned around and saw Henley and Edison do the same. She leaned forward and wrapped her arms around its neck as natural as if she had been horseback riding her whole life, which she hadn't. The falcon twisted its neck and winked before beginning a steady climb up into the sky. Her eyes remained shut as she fought off her fear and paranoia. The air was so thin she knew magic must be at play—no human could breathe at this altitude. Past the clouds, through the wisps, they moved for what felt like hours as the sun beat down on them. Her heart plunged to her stomach when the falcon began its descent and dropped into a sharp, deep dive before hovering in a gentle circular motion. She surveyed the birds, hoping to make eye contact with Edison and Henley, but her eyes were drawn to the trees. A whole box of crayon colors in all the shades nature had to offer—a most beautiful and a welcome sight.

Her falcon escort whispered, "Directly beneath us is Katamoor, the most sacred place on our planet. The Virago

Trees house our Spirits. We'll stop now, just for a moment." And Parker wondered if all birds on Spyridon spoke English so well. She was awe-struck by the rich emerald color in the midst of the whiteness of the cloud layers. They looked like a kind of Mangrove tree and were the largest trees she had seen in her lifetime, with strong and forceful limbs twisting and curling in the first shot of bright color in the Upperworld. She had traveled the forests of America, through the magnificent redwoods, and had never encountered anything with the scale and power of these Virago Trees. Neon lime-colored leaves ignited with luscious sparkling red veins rose to kiss the clouds. Something about the trees emitted an electrified energy, and instinctively, Parker knew she didn't want to make contact with the trees.

"Let your eyes roam our forest," the falcon said. "Katamoor is the largest and last remaining continent on Spyridon. It covers fifteen percent of our planet's surface. It belongs to the Upperworld and is the home to our Virago Trees, our lifeline."

Parker gasped as her eyes focused on the vision below, which became even more exaggerated. She stared in wonder at the magic of this keen heightened sense of sight and gazed in awe that on this planet she was experiencing eagle-eye vision. Sort of like the way birds on Earth pick up the tiniest grain of food from their heights in the sky. The marshy wetlands stretched for miles and miles, until the land mass met with a white-capped sea. As the land greenery refined even more, and her sight sharpened,

Parker's body began to vibrate and shake. Electric currents ran through her. Her falcon guide grabbed her closer, forcing her to relax.

"Our Virago Trees have prevailed through the evolution of the planet, the Great War, and the whims of the Spirits. You are feeling their power."

"Glad you said something, I was getting a little worried."

Impossible to conceive of a planet the size of Earth with only one land mass. Yet, here was a continent with a forest of Mangroves. Far from typical ones. From her studies, Parker knew Mangroves survived and thrived in the most stringent conditions, even hot, muddy, salty waters that would quickly kill most trees and plants.

"I have to ask—how do these trees give you everything you need—all the necessary resources for an entire planet of birds?"

"Ahhh, yes, one of our greatest mysteries we can only attribute to our cultural beliefs. Our Spirits have taken care of us. They ensure we endure. Though of late, we have been at a loss to understand what has happened to our waters."

"Why, what happened?"

"We're not sure." The falcon appeared sad, perhaps even frightened. "Our people have been inexplicably getting sick. We've narrowed it down to our water sources. We just pray our environment is safe. We pray often."

Then, as quickly as the falcon stopped, the five falcons joined together at their wing tips and rapidly evolved to perform what appeared to be a ceremonial dance. They spun in the air while making their distinguished, repetitive ee-chup calls. Parker, Edison and Henley grasped onto the massive chests of their falcons. When they finished swirling in the air, each falcon separated and seemed refreshed.

Parker asked, "What were you doing?"

"We do not pass by Katamoor without offering gratitude and respect. The falcon signaled to his group and swiveled his neck to face Parker. "Now back to the Citadel, the Sky King's castle. We promised the Ruling Great One a swift return. It is almost dusk, and we are cutting it close, the presentation begins sharply at sundown."

With that, they ascended into the air for the return flight to the Sky Box. Parker's stomach was still in her mouth. She wanted to feel her feet back on the ground, rubbery though it might be.

chapter six

They stood in a pool of brilliant light on a wooden stage. Belliza flittered back and forth impatiently, appearing to address all of them, or one of them; it was unclear. The dialogue came out in one explosive, rambling run-on sentence.

"You're to be introduced to the Great Onez, of course, az zaviorz of the planet, becauze tonight iz a very zpecial night, and we hope to zelebrate the beginning of the end of our troublez, no more toxic water, no zhortage of clean water, no more food zcarzity, everything goez perfectly, no more dark mutteringz, a bright future becauze of you three heroez!"

Parker opened her mouth to begin a long line of questions, but the flighty little thing had disappeared. Wonderful.

She was not a great fan of the spotlight, for obvious reasons. Public spectacles horrified her, to be frank.

"How much of that did you understand?" Parker asked Edison and Henley.

Henley flashed a 'don't mess with me' expression, and said, "Stefanos went over this already. Great Ones, humph, they parade us around like a trio of peacocks."

She gave Edison, and definitely not Parker, the arched eyebrow.

"I see what you did there. Good one," Edison said.

Henley went on, to Edison. "In the what else would they call it category, duh, the Great Hall. I guess everything is great here. Especially us."

"So, we're on stage, and I get the feeling we're gonna be the stars of the show," Edison said. "Let's see the gratitude Stefanos kept talking about."

Parker smiled, at least they're joking and somewhat optimistic, even if her companions sounded sarcastic. Better than hostile, she thought, though she already figured she would have to work hard to be included.

Or not. She'd lived on the margins long enough to know how to deal.

"You're not fooling anyone," she muttered half to herself. "You need them, idiot."

"You say something?" Henley asked, with the usual amount of snark.

Great big sigh. "No."

"Feel free to keep it that way."

The stage was centered in a cavernous amphitheater in the round. Rows upon rows of horizontal wooden poles circled the room—from the base of the stage to the height of the auditorium. Parker guessed the poles must be perches for the leaders.

The clammy tropical climate saturated Parker's body with an ocean of perspiration. She glanced at Edison and Henley—both sweating profusely too. What she wouldn't give for a cold blast of a Nor'easter right now.

Deafening caws and shrieks resounded at once. Henley covered her ears. Parker turned toward the entry where flocks of birds lined up. The parade of species filed into the room. Parker watched in awe and shock as all shapes and sizes of the human-like birds settled onto the perches. She wondered if the birds had assigned places as they moved toward their perches with polite and courteous human-like movements.

Her mind, prone to the scientific, quickly started to categorize. Just as Stefanos had described, most had human characteristics like arms, hands, legs, and feet, though many sported talons. Some had large noses and mouths in place of beaks. A few even wore clothing—from colorful ornamental robes to simple sheaths of fabric similar to the sacks she, Edison, and Henley wore. Many had vivid, brightly colored feathers, tropical in appearance, while others' plumages were more somber in gray and neutral tones. Some towered as large as twelve to fifteen feet tall like Stefanos, while others were as diminutive and tiny as Belliza. But all in the Upperworld shared the dark, glowing marble eyes.

Taking in the scene before her, Parker weakened at the knees. She scanned the auditorium hoping to find Stefanos or Belliza. She tried to tell herself she could do this but convincing herself was a long way off.

Henley wore a pained expression. Her hands cemented to her ears. She cringed and leaned in toward Edison. Parker couldn't make out what she was saying. Henley held on to her snotty attitude, but not as nasty. She still directed her words mostly to Edison but she said them loud enough so Parker wouldn't miss them, "The smell is gross, I don't even want to breathe."

Parker rolled her eyes, not finding the smell gross at all.

The lights dimmed, and Parker side-eyed her companions. Shaking, they held hands in solidarity. Not moving. Their eyes focused on one another. She wished Edison would reach out to her with his free hand and bring her into their circle.

Parker's summer at the teens' program at the American Museum of Natural History had provided a lot of insight about the avian world. She knew birds were hard-wired to think and communicate with one another, even with humans. She thought back to how she had described to Henley about the proportion of a bird's brain being similar to the ratio of the human brain to the body. Though birds appeared slight, they were remarkably strong. Henley may have called her a nerd, but this bird culture was beginning to make more sense. If parrots could vocalize, so why not all birds? She'd even read how birds can problem-solve like humans and have a human kind of memory that distinguishes between intention and desire. She even remembered some birds, like the Weavers and Crows, are so smart they have been known to design and make tools.

At the NYU workshop last fall, when she had studied the evolution of different species, the professor had engaged them in an intense debate. Had the most advantageous attributes grown proportionately through use, over time? Had the less useful body parts atrophied and diminished in size? Even though the Sky King's head had grown large enough to support a highly developed brain, Belliza exemplified the perfect specimen to disprove a large head wasn't necessary for human level sapience.

Parker often mused future generations would morph into big heads on top of small bodies with larger hands and arms for holding hand-held devices. All related to the overuse of technology. Her dad used to joke that the cell phone would finish off civilization as they knew it!

She hurt just thinking about him now.

A hushed silence took over the Great Hall. Heads and beaks tilted upward as Stefanos appeared at the height of the room with the majesty of a respected leader. Draped in an embroidered white satin flowing cloak, Stefanos rose among his leaders, his wings filling the stage. He ascended to a golden perch suspended from the top of the Great Hall's ceiling.

"Tonight, we welcome to our planet our esteemed guests from the planet Earth. They will be our emissaries and they will help us achieve sustainability. We will teach them the powers of our people," Stefanos continued. "We will share our gifts and they will share their knowledge. And through this process, we will improve our planet—and hopefully the universe."

Sizzling explosives whistled in the backdrop and triggered Parker's memories of the Fourth of July fireworks on the East River. She had feared them as a child and the same feelings crept over her now. Somewhere in her head, she believed what Stefanos said—they were on a mission of goodness. Maybe the fireworks signified a celebration related to their arrival?

No. Something's wrong. A number of the bird people took flight in a panic.

Bursts of orange and red fire filled the space, followed by dense, smoke-laden clouds. Parker narrowed her eyes attempting to slice through the smoke. The Great Ones' feathers fluttered, and their wings flapped in frenzied motion. A flurry of quills spilled across the towering space. An uproar of distraught bird calls filled the Great Hall. Smoke swirled about the stage and blazing sparks ignited in one of the corners. The smell of flames mixed with the odor of scorched feathers and burned through the air. This was not a celebration.

Henley screamed, "OMG! How stupid are we? We're going to be killed!"

White ribbons of charred gasses climbed high to the top of the Great Hall. The surrounding walls weakened and in places vaporized. Each jolt trembled the perches. Thrusts of air quivered the fortress and all its limbs. Another loud crash. The Great Hall slewed to one side, throwing Parker off her feet. Within, the Great Ones swayed with each explosive burst as the Citadel in the Sky shook and vibrated as if a sinking ship on the verge of capsizing.

Most of the Great Ones remained frozen in place. Those who had survived and were able to move sought an exit path and scattered, flying to safety from the fire and smoky debris.

High above her, Parker felt Stefanos's gaze. Suddenly, he was upon her, swooping through the flames and onto the stage. A large bleeding gash stood out red beside one eye. He flew to her side and gathered all three of them together in his wings.

chapter seven

The barrage of blasts had ceased. The grayness of the air hung with the sober reminder the Upperworld had been attacked. Parker's throat burned. The smell of death and decay choked out most of her faith that there would be a good outcome on this planet.

Parker lay flat on her back, sinking into the floor's cushiony softness. Stefanos had deposited them back in the place where she'd started her journey, the floating complex.

She closed her eyes and wondered if her lashes still lined her eyelids, or had they been permanently fried by the heat. She prayed she was sleeping and would wake up feverish in bed from this nightmare. The odor, the air, and the sinking of her heart couldn't be blocked out—this would not turn into the remnants of a bad dream. Light-headed, Parker willed herself to sit up and find her equilibrium. More importantly, where were Henley and Edison?

"Edison—Henley!" Parker rasped as she called out. "Where are you?" Cries and moans pulsed in the background. Parker swallowed hard and raised her voice, "Henley! Edison! Can you hear me? Are you alright?"

"I think I'm alive," Edison said, his voice trembling. "I'm not sure I want to be though. What happened to us?"

Parker, blinded by the thick smoke, couldn't see in front of her and could barely distinguish the murmur of Edison's voice. She answered, "No clue. But are you alright? You didn't get burned, did you? Or hit by anything?"

"No. I'm okay. As good as I can be, considering." His voice cracked and his words spit out between fits of coughing. "Parker, I'm going to move to your voice. If you keep talking, maybe I can find you."

"Henley? Henley?" Parker called. "Answer me!" Tears streamed down her cheeks. "Please tell me you are okay." Henley didn't answer. Parker felt someone crawling toward her. She brought her knees to her chest in a fetal position, closing her body to protect herself. But as the figure neared, she recognized Henley—her face streaked with blood and her beautiful black mane wet and covered in soot—limp from the heat. Parker extended her arms to pull Henley in close, but the girl pushed her away.

The old eagle neared her.

"Stefanos!" Parker said, "What is going on? You said this was a night of celebration? Why would you be attacked like this? Who would do this to you?"

"I wish I could answer your questions, Parker, but this is all very unexpected," he said, with a calm she didn't believe. Stefanos tipped his beak and motioned toward a gaping, blackened tunnel fifty feet ahead of them. "We shall find who is responsible for the attack, but for now your safety is of paramount importance. The location of the Sky Box is not known to many. No harm can come to you there. Thankfully, our Weavers from Kokobur designed it to be indestructible. I'm taking you there now."

His strong voice softened, and he murmured, as if to himself, "Since the last war, we thought we would never require it again." His heavy brow furrowed, but he quickly shook it off.

"My thoughts are with you now. You carry the aftermath of the shock in your bodies. I know you have never experienced anything like this. The attack appears to be over."

"You put us in the middle of a war!" Henley demanded. "You owe us an explanation!"

"We will talk when I return. I must go to my Roost and meet with my advisors. The assault has stopped and the Upperworld is safe for the time being. As are you. I am grateful to the Spirits of the Sky—they have watched out for us tonight."

Stefanos fingered the medallion hanging from his neck and broke into a melody of trills, and calls. "You are extraordinary earthlings. You have been blessed with heightened intelligence. Beyond your years. It is why you have been selected. It is also why you stayed. Your choice did not surprise me, but I am grateful for your decisions. Now we will help each of you discover all that you are."

Stefanos, for the second time, whispered directly into

her mind. "Take your time with your companions. They need you now. I trust you will find your way with them."

A trail of sparrows appeared out of the darkness. They carried cool, damp cloths in their beaks, brushed past each of them, clearing their eyes and cleaning the soot from their faces. The sparrows made a speedy exit from the Sky Box, as quickly and quietly as they entered. Henley and Edison neared one another and sat together on the opposite side of the room away from her. Parker steeled herself, wishing she could join their conversation. But just like at school, with their backs to her, they communicated stay away without a word.

She approached them. "Uh, I'm glad you two are okay." Parker swallowed hard, building her courage to continue.

Edison and Henley locked eyes before acknowledging her. She didn't know if they'd figured out about the telepathic communication or not or felt like Stefanos had singled her out as more important than them. She needed them. They needed her.

"Whatever you are thinking, whatever you think of me, let's put it aside because we are stuck in this together," Parker said.

"Really? Cuz things aren't as they appear then," Henley flipped back. "He told you something, didn't he?"

"Nothing. I think he wanted to get back to his leaders. Nothing else. I think he's giving us time to, umm, I guess to recover." Parker bit her lip and forced herself to say, "Can we please be friends?" She knew she must sound like a kid in nursery school begging to share toys. But what else could she say?

"We don't need to be friends, Parker. But I'll give you this, we're here to do a job. Save this planet. As long as you are straight up with us, we'll get along. Cuz you're not the only one with brains. I have some of my own ideas how we can help here." Henley pointed at Edison and said, "And so does he."

In her own way, Henley was giving her an opening. She'd take it. They didn't have to like each other.

"I'll say it again. You know what I know. Belliza mentioned a water shortage, and an ecological disaster. The falcons too. They brought us here because of it. Stefanos is protecting us because he does need us."

"And they think that's going to happen with somebody trying to blow us up!" Henley shouted. "Parker, how can you focus on some stupid water shortage when someone's trying to kill us?"

Edison's sweet humming calmed Henley again. She leaned against the wall, flopped onto the floor, pushed her legs out in front of her, and quieted down.

Parker flopped herself down on the cushiony floor. "I remember the first time I saw Belliza." She figured she'd tell her story and maybe lure them to tell theirs.

Henley snorted.

Edison spoke up, "Hey Henley, let's hear her out."

"Belliza kept coming to my window. For months. And she just hung out there, in the sky, staring at me. At first, I wondered if it was the same bird. But weird, right? I thought a tiny little bird like that, eighteen stories up in the air on my balcony. I checked out the behavior of hummingbirds, and unless they are migrating, they hang low, near the flowers and bushes. They just don't buzz around exploring at the height of buildings in New York City, especially in the winter. Or really anywhere."

"Jeez, is there anything you don't know?" Henley said, rolling her eyeballs and adding, "I just knew it! Is that all you do, research Google?"

Parker's mind snapped like a taut rubber band back to bio lab and the incident with Jason Bender. After Dr. Stillman complimented her in front of the whole class on her perfect dissection of a frog's liver, Jason ran through the halls at Tate calling her the "organ bandit". No one would go near her for weeks. Parker steadied herself, refusing to be baited.

"So, this little bird is at my window just about every day whenever my parents weren't around. I knew it had to be the same one because of her markings—the perfect black triangle between the eyes and white-tipped tail feathers seemed pretty distinct. I knew from school birds' feather colorations are almost like human fingerprints—no two are identical."

Another snort of derision out of Henley, and a dark chuckle.

"Wait—it gets even stranger. The bird is circling back and forth, motioning to me to come outside and on to the ledge. I'm scratching my head at this point because I'm getting a weird feeling. This is the craziest thing that ever happened to me. Even crazier, I felt like the bird was trying to tell me something. So, I opened the door to go out on the terrace. I'm wondering what the bird could possibly want from me. But in some way, I know something is going down and it feels off. Like a bird trying to communicate with its eyes. Hmmm, it's the last thing I remember. And I woke up here."

Edison gasped. "You're scaring me now. Why would you respond to a bird, outside, so high up in a building? That's kinda nuts! You could have fallen. Then, you'd be dead. And we'd be dead now too!"

"No way, Eddie! We are alive," Henley broke in, not letting the convo go on without her. "You saw all those other kids here just like us. They came and they left. We decided to stay. We have nothing to lose. We go back to Earth and no one knows we've been gone. We're on an adventure. More exciting than stupid school at home!"

Parker jumped in, "Well, I agree with you Henley on one thing—we are alive. But when did you guys first see Belliza? A bunch of times, too, like me?"

"No, I don't think I saw her again—just multiple times on one day," Edison said. "But she kept playing tricks on me, right after my choir practice. So, I'm waiting for my brother, Ozzie, to finish his basketball game so we could walk home together. The streets are pretty dark at night where we live. It's safer to have my brother with me. I checked my phone, and Ozzie hadn't texted me, so I began to head home alone.

"The timing was so weird though. I just got this ring."

He extended his hand to Henley and Parker exposing his ring finger with its hefty onyx and gold signet band. "Everyone who gets into the choir gets one. And I remember I'm just staring at it when I noticed the bird."

"It's beautiful, Edison." Parker held his hand for a closer view.

He took in a breath. "It's the sign of the dove. Peace. Ha! Now the whole bird thing..." He shook his head without finishing.

Parker could have sworn with his athletic physique, he belonged on a competitive sports team. Didn't figure him as a choir boy. Embarrassed, she quickly chastised herself. She didn't like being judged on appearances. Why was she doing this to him? How someone looks is not who they are.

"I'm standing outside our church," Edison said with a half-smile, "so happy cuz I made the cut to go to the national competition. It's a big deal. That's when this buzzing sound went flying over my head. I thought it might be an insect or something. I tried to wave it away, but the bird kept following me down the street. So irritating!"

His eyes darted to Henley, her back still propped up against the glass, feet stretched out on the floor. She nodded to him, encouraging him to continue.

"So, this tiny thing comes flying at me, like a baseball over home plate. You're either going to hit the ball hard and send it out of the park, or you're gonna duck and get out of the way because it's comin' so fast. But again, just the dumb bird. When I saw the long skinny beak and the triangle mark, I figured it must be a hummingbird. And definitely not a species we have anywhere near Detroit." He side-eyed Henley apologetically, "Trust me, now don't go calling me an Audubon expert—I'm not! Far from it!"

Henley grinned and Parker couldn't believe he got her to crack a smile.

"Next I feel a sharp poke in my back, and I'm spooked cuz it could be a kid with a knife or something. Like I said, sometimes it's not safe on the streets around where I live. But it was only the bird—jabbing its beak into my back.

"I'm all nerved up and this bird's making me crazy. It's swirling in front of me. I'm getting dizzy and the last thing I remember, I'm crossing the street. A big dark SUV is heading right at me. The brakes screech and then boom. I'm in a dark tunnel of jelly and wake up here.

"So now do you get where I'm going, why I think we might be dead? You know how you hear the stories of people who come back to life after they've had some kinda near-death experience. They're in a dark tunnel and there's a light at the end of it? Well, I come through a dark tunnel and end up in this bright white-hot room. So, could we be dead?" Edison asked.

Parker stole another glance at Henley, who tapped her foot while flicking her finger with her thumb. Parker realized Henley teetered on the edge, wanting to spill her story, but holding herself back.

And something else. Another similarity to Edison's story and hers. Edison had just accomplished something— he'd made the choir cut. She knew of those competitions.

They were tough.

Parker wavered, unsure whether or not she should tell them the great news she received on the same day. Her guidance counselor had called her into her office to tell her she was the first Tate student to receive an Early Acceptance decision from John Hopkins. She had planned on surprising her parents when they returned from work, so happy and proud she was on her way to becoming a scientist. And now, what?

Subject of an attempted assassination plot? Potential hero?

She blushed and finally blurted, "I had something really good happen to me that day, too. You guys already figured out I've been a nerd my whole life. But it's weird, on the day we got here, I was offered a position in the Future Scholars Program at John Hopkins. And you got into the choir, Edison. Something we both worked so hard for and wanted so badly."

A sudden yawn gripped her. Good lord, she hadn't slept in ages. She couldn't be sure how much time had passed, but the day felt unseasonably long, like those videos of the sun slowly circling the sky during winter in the Arctic Circle. She felt the crash reverberate through the rest of her body.

"I'm sorry… I need to get some sleep." She was a firm believer in early to bed and early to rise.

"It's fine," Edison told her, while Henley rolled her eyes and muttered something unintelligible. "We'll stay up a bit more and get some shuteye also."

The main room had a short hallway, followed by a number of smaller, empty rooms separated by beaded curtains without any of the beads, made of the same soft fabric as her shift. The good news was the floor felt like it would be perfect to sleep on.

She didn't get a chance to lay down, because suddenly a familiar, sweet aroma surrounded her.

"Good going, Parker." The hummingbird buzzed in front of Parker and whisked her to another small room. "I zee zome progrezz with your companionz. I think you have even inzpired Henley."

"Why are you moving me without my permission? Please don't do that. I want to stay with Edison and Henley."

"Zeemz Henley doez like to tangle with you." Belliza laughed with the gentle sound of a tease. A portion of the wall before Parker lit up, with a nearly transparent view of Henley and Edison chatting. Edison had crossed the room over to Henley and sat beside her—his back now leaning against the wall next to her, mimicking her position. He looked over his shoulder and shook his head.

"How are you handling all this?" he asked. "As well as Parker?"

"I wish she'd disappear. Then maybe we'd have a chance to get out of here."

"Forget about her, Henley. We gotta deal with the situation in front of us. Do you think we're dead?"

"I dunno. Right now, I think it might be better than being alive in this bird sanctuary."

"Don't say that!" He grimaced. They were silent for a few seconds, but to Parker watching them on screen, the absence of sound passed like an hour.

"What *did* happen to you? How did you get here?" Edison asked, lowering his voice to a hush.

Parker peered through the glass as if watching actors on stage playing out some fictionalized version of their lives. "Belliza, can't they tell there's a camera? We're watching them."

"They can't zee us. Only we can zee them."

"I have no idea how I got here," Henley said. "But, like you, I saw the hummingbird bird only one day before I ended up here. I did hear it droning on and on. I was outside on our patio concentrating on my submission for the Intel Science and Engineering Fair. It was the day we ended up here. I remembered because the bird's beak kept messing with my laptop and I was worried it would take a crap on my screen. But later on, I was out and heading home and it's stalking me.

"I swatted it away, but it came back for more, tracking me for a couple hundred feet, all the way up my driveway. It started to get aggressive. And I was losing my cool and getting mad. I guess, you've seen me do that. Ha!" She laughed and continued. "And the bird flew right in front of my head, buzzed around and touched my arm, and I lost it!

"I started to chase it away. I stumbled to the edge of our driveway and took a tough fall. It's kinda dark around my house at night, too, and the canyons drop off pretty steep. I got up and the bird flew back in my face and threw me off my feet. I dropped my backpack, and I'm desperate now, so I grabbed onto a little sparse tree. The limb broke and last thing I remember, I am hanging over the edge of the canyon. I must have passed out."

Edison gaped while cracking his knuckles. He rubbed his fingers over his hands, and said, "Then, we must be dead."

Belliza buzzed into Parker's right ear, "I azzure you, Parker. You are all very much alive."

chapter eight

The night passed with a distressing quickness. It felt as though she'd gotten about two hours of sleep before sunlight woke her again. The blackness of the night had come and gone with a finger snap. So swiftly, it had dissolved abruptly into the full light of day.

From the looks of things, Henley and Edison weren't doing any better. They shuffled into the common room bleary-eyed and muttering obscenities at the morning.

Stefanos approached on soundless wings, the bloody gash on his head had been wrapped in an eye patch.

Following the Sky King, a flock of small sparrows toted woven baskets of seeds and grains in their beaks. The wisp of wall opened with the slight motion of the Sky King's wingtip and Parker and Belliza floated into the Sky Box along with the sparrows. Parker and Henley sniffed the baskets suspiciously and turned their heads. Edison grabbed a handful of seeds and tossed them into his mouth. Parker was starving, though not enough to be tempted to experiment with the rations.

"I'm not hungry," she said mostly to herself. Henley added, "Me neither." Edison didn't stand on ceremony and dug his hand into the basket, throwing a few more big handfuls into his mouth.

"You will be. On Spyridon, I can assure you, Parker and Henley, it will take more than a hearty meal to keep you strong," the Sky King said without breaking his stare.

She waited for Stefanos to speak again. Her thoughts drew her home to her father's teasing. Whenever she stopped talking, her father would make her feel better by saying, "When I negotiate, I learned 'he who speaks first loses'. Are you playing that game with me?"

Parker didn't plan to lose.

He touched the tip of his wing to the soft feathers of his white beard. "We are still sorting out what happened last night. I have organized my leaders and regional troops to search the Citadel for any evidence."

"You told us our arrival would be celebrated," Henley said. "Seems to me the event felt more like the celebration of our death."

The sparrows, startled by her tone, dropped their baskets and fled the room.

"I understand your thinking, Henley. But what happened was not our doing. But we will find out and we will have answers. We were as blind-sided as you." He put on a thinking face and drew closer to them. "I do owe you an explanation. So please listen. We have spoken much about Spyridon and the Upperworld. But we have not spoken of the Underworld and life below the Spyridon Sea."

Parker opened her mouth to ask a question. Stefanos circled his wings and motioned for her to be still. He continued, "The world above the Spyridon Sea is ours. All below the sea belongs to the Underworld. We have maintained a separate, and sometimes, uneasy peace with the Underworld. The boundaries between our worlds have not been crossed. We live without the benefit of the Underworld resources. And they live without the benefit of our resources.

"More than twenty years have passed since we have battled. We waged war on the Underworld then. And we won. This assault does not make sense to any of us. The current leadership of the Underworld, Empress Diadora and her brother, Commanding General Pantione, want to maintain their own status quo. They are not interested in us, our problems, or in collaborating with us in any way. They live their lives below the sea. We live ours above the sea. We just want to survive and live out our days peacefully." He sighed and with sadness said, "Now we will be forced to find out if the Underworld plotted the attack. Personally, I pray this did not come from them.

"A few months before your arrival, we noticed toxicity in our waters. At first, we thought it natural causes, brought about by the environmental damage. But after testing, we found traces of poison. We are gaining clarity every day and learned we are suffering at the hands of evil. A very clever, very careful evil. One we cannot pinpoint. That is why we called for you. We are grateful you three have chosen to help us. We believe you have the knowledge we lack to fix our problems."

Parker brimmed with questions and interrupted him. "You can bring us to your planet from the other side of the universe. Why can't you bring the resources you need from Earth? You are capable of moving anything. Why not bring from other planets the things your people need to survive."

"Spyridon is our home. Our culture dictates our planet must sustain us. In our distant past, we were frivolous, and we took all we could. We took until the near destruction of everything and everyone on our planet. It is a mistake we will not repeat. We will live here and thrive on our planet's own resources. And you three will help us.

"We go to my Roost now and you will meet my closest advisors. You are part of our inner circle. It is the only way you can help us. You must know everything."

They rose into the air and floated behind him. They wove through the wispy walls of the Citadel until they stopped in midair before a smaller glass room which also rose high above the clouds.

"Welcome to my Roost. We can see all of the Upperworld from here," Stefanos said. "My Tribunal meets here. I find the weight of our decisions often lingers. Perhaps you feel the Spirits' presence in this room?"

Stefanos nudged them toward a peculiar-looking, elderly hawkish bird Parker hadn't noticed when she first flew into the Roost. The hawk had positioned himself within the shadows of a swirl of smoggy mist that swept the corners of the small room. Parker gathered the Sky King's

Roost was a sort of turret—a place to keep an eye on his kingdom.

"Come away from the mist, Great Vibius. I'd prefer you greet our guests appropriately. Makes me think you don't want us to find you?"

"You joke with me, Ruling Great One. Your eyesight is far better than any of ours—wearing an eye patch or not," he laughed. "I don't mean to joke with you, Sky King. Do you feel alright? How did you get hit by the cross-fire?"

Stefanos chuckled and said, "It takes more than a ball of fire to stop me." He threw his wings around the old hawk. "Yes, my eyes will always find you, Great Vibius. I do joke—but perhaps our guests here will get the wrong impression. We don't want to startle them." He used his wing to move the old hawk closer to the earthlings and continued, "Great Vibius, you have not had the pleasure of meeting our earthlings. This is Parker Kittredge, Henley Wang and Edison Baker."

Parker repeated the old hawk's name to herself, hoping to remember. Her memory often lapsed when it came to names, especially these odd names that seemed centuries old and belonged to these bizarre creatures.

"Meet my cousin, Great Vibius. My close advisor and a member of my Tribunal. And most importantly, my dear friend. Come give them an appropriate welcome, Vibius! They won't bite," he teased. "Unless, you do first!"

Stepping out of the cloud of fog, the elderly hawk appeared a little younger than Stefanos. Fewer craggy crevices. He, too, had to be quite old though and she wondered why he was uncomfortable greeting them. Because they were earthlings? His over-sized head sported a ragged crest pointed like a black flame on top.

Stefanos stroked his white beard. "Show our guests here you are happy to meet them. The concern you wear has nothing to do with them." He tipped his beak as if to consider probing further, but he restrained himself. "You know I play with you, Great Vibius. Don't you? A little levity can't hurt us."

"I do not see the humor today Sky King," Vibius said. "At first, I was curious, as were all our Great Ones, about the display of lights and fireworks last evening. But now, with the knowledge of the attack and the loss of so many lives…" His voice hesitated. "Well, laughter does not seem appropriate." He turned toward the earthlings, then back to Stefanos. "May I speak candidly in front of our visitors?"

"Of course," Stefanos said. "Or, they would not be here."

"We haven't had any pushback from the Underworld in near twenty years. If this is a real threat of war, as it appears, there is no humor."

Stefanos turned his gaze to observe the canyons of blue sky veiled in clouds and mist spreading before them in endless succession. He rubbed the medallion around his neck. Parker recalled the bronze piece from the first time they met. An eagle wearing an ornament had seemed odd. Now as he touched it, the piece appeared perfectly fitting suspended from his collar of feathers, above his heart.

Stefanos leaned in, bringing them close together. "We have no reason to claim the assault came from the Underworld. No proof points to them." He paused before serving up his last word, "Yet."

"Maybe they have just had enough, Great Sky King. Maybe they knew our humans were introduced last night and they chose our celebration to make their point."

"And what point would that be?"

"They will not stand by any longer and let us keep the world above the sea to ourselves. Someone or something is out to destroy us. Masses of our people died during last night's attack. Out of nowhere! No warning! And this assault—it comes right after we discovered our waters have been poisoned. Our people are sick and dying from the tainted waters across our regions. This is no coincidence. We cannot live without clean water. If it is not the Underworld, who could it be? And if it is them—we cannot be their prey."

"Of course, I agree. But we will not make a unilateral decision until we have all the facts. We will find the culprits, and we will act when we are prepared. I will not pass judgment until then," Stefanos said.

Parker's body vibrated an electric buzzing sound and Stefanos appeared distracted. At first, thinking the buzz came from Belliza, Parker stole a quick look—but the hummingbird hadn't moved or spoken. The distracting noise continued until Stefanos said, "I just received a communication from Cole. He is on his way from the Underworld. I am anxious to learn what he has to say."

Parker squinted her eyes, perplexed a Great One could be a member of his Tribunal and belong to the Underworld.

"I understand your confusion, Parker. Cole is an Upperworlder. A limited few of us can live in both worlds. Those with royal blood and oddly enough, those of you from Earth, until the age of twenty-one. The environments in which we live on Spyridon have dictated the path of our separate and distinct form of evolution. Cole is a bit of an anomaly. In fact, you will see Cole is far more human in his appearance than the rest of us. He came to us from Earth as a mere child." Stefanos eyes twinkled.

Stefanos angled his neck toward the direction of the opening to the Roost. The room brightened and Stefanos opened his wings to embrace the attractive young man who entered. Parker thought he appeared mostly human—but his skin had a light feathering which gave the appearance of fine blonde hair.

Shorter than Stefanos or Vibius, Cole must have been nearly a full head taller than she, close to seven feet, and about her age, too. Brilliant, piercing blue eyes flashed under a head of thick blonde hair. His wings neatly tucked into a lean muscular fame. He could have passed for an earthling with the exception of those wings. He wore a black and golden feathered vest and Parker wondered if the vest served as a symbol he belonged to the Upperworld.

"Did you receive my transmission, Great Sky King?" Cole asked, "You didn't acknowledge it." He stopped. "I am sure Diadora and Pantione did not plan this assault."

Stefanos relaxed his wingspan and embraced Cole. "Ah, I am glad you are here. I trust your journey from the Underworld went smoothly." His wing remained on Cole's shoulder. "We are all aware this has been a difficult night. I've called a meeting with the Great Ones. There must be no dissent among us. We need a unified front on our next steps."

Parker admired Stefanos' respectful manner. He spoke to Cole and Vibius as equals. Even though he was the Ruling Great One, Parker sensed his leadership yielded to collaboration. Her father had said there is only one way to get things done: work as a team, regardless of how diverse or subordinate the teammates are.

"Are you certain those slippery fish are blameless?" Vibius asked.

"They are the only enemy known to us," Stefanos agreed.

"It is not my intention," Cole said, "to argue with you, Great Sky King. But I am in the Underworld every day. Their concern is with their own survival and strengthening their world, not endangering ours. That's how it has been since first I took up my post. They do not seek to harm us. These environmental issues are not the result of orders coming from the Underworld leaders. Planning a strike, tainting our waters—none of it is possible! If they were involved with the poisonings, they would be condemning themselves to a war—a war they are far from certain of winning." Vibius strode forward. "Great Cole, you have infiltrated their world. You have provided invaluable information we would not have otherwise. You are as close to the royal family of the Underworld as is physically possible. But we must ask, just in case, is it conceivable they have tricked us? Is it possible they have discovered your allegiance to the Sky King and have played us all?"

A fresh pang of danger flared in Parker's chest. Cole—a double agent. Given his role soaking up intelligence from this Underworld and their people, and then, disseminating false information to them, his life must have been a constant walk along the edge of a knife.

Stefanos raised the medallion to his heart and softly but firmly said, "I will ensure the boundaries between the Upperworld and the Underworld are separate and not to be navigated. We will continue life as we know it and there will be peace. That must never change. But, as the protectors of the Upperworld, we must maintain our rule of Spyridon and all access to our planet and points beyond. We will step up our guard of all portals and protect our passages.

The more they spoke, the more worried Parker became about the future. Stefanos had told them there had been humans here before and they returned to Earth, and no one knew they were missing. But if Cole came as a young child, and remained, was it simply he chose not to return at all?

What if, like Cole, she grew wings and could never return to her old life?

"Great Cole, poll your comrades below the sea and listen carefully to each of them for what you can uncover. Anything untoward or even unsaid. Anything that doesn't ring true about last night. I want a thorough investigation. Our funerals will take place tomorrow in The Woods by the South Gate. The families of our lost leaders deserve answers. And they shall have them. Be present, be involved, and for the sake of all of us, act normally around Pantione and Diadora."

The golden young man took his leave and hadn't even acknowledged her presence. She blushed, wondering why she had hoped he would give her a quick look.

"Parker, you have observed my vision can penetrate great distances—rock, or wood or metal." Stefanos said. "But there is only one place where my eyes are blocked— the Underworld of Spyridon. Not even one inch below the water. I worry about what I can't see. And that is where Cole comes in. He is my eyes —below the sea."

chapter nine

What first struck Parker were the sounds of mourning. Bird cries and wails easily distinguished themselves from happy chirping and it broke her heart. The sound accompanied their journey from the moment Belliza had picked them up in the Sky Box, just as the dark of the night enveloped the day. The howls followed them through the blackness to the South Gate. Parker burst into tears and as soon as she recovered, the tears poured out of her again. The sadness seemed to haunt Edison and Henley. None of them spoke.

After a lengthy flight, they hovered above another canyon of darkness, not dissimilar to the North Gate where they had said their goodbyes to the teens who chose to return to Earth. As they stood on the cloud's edge, the wind cut through them with a hot rush of fear and the uncomfortable sensation of floating on a cloud supported with a base of reeds and twigs.

Parker thought she recognized the haunting hoots of owls.

"Did you guys hear that?" she asked. She concentrated harder to understand the cryptic weeping sounds of mourning rising through the air. The canyon rim glowed in a circle of fire. From the air, the vast stretch of emptiness appeared the size of a small city, almost the way the island of Manhattan might look from the window seat of a plane. Every few feet a fire burned.

Stefanos emerged from the darkness, Vibius at his side. Together they floated to the highest point on the edge of the canyons. The glow of a great fire illuminated the Sky King so all could visualize their leader. He held his beak toward the sky, demonstrating his strength and honor.

At the canyon's base, great mounds of wooden sticks and logs wove into tangled webs, filling the entirety of the giant valley far below the Citadel. They had referred to the base of the Citadel as The Woods at the South Gate. Ahh, so these were a larger version of the protruding jumble of wooden sticks that she had seen at the bottom of the passing clouds. They must have formed the intricate foundation the clouds rested upon.

Parker watched shapes, barely visible, moving and weaving beneath them in a circular progression. Funerals were the hardest to bear. But a mass funeral like this pierced her soul. Stefanos wore a black hooded cloak, obscuring his head in its shadow. As they moved closer to the rim, Parker could see all the Great Ones dressed similarly, faceless behind the cloaks without distinction between leaders or their people. The Upperworld mourned privately. Parker's vision sharpened as she took in the piles of bodies. At least twenty leaf-wrapped bodies stacked one upon the other layered in each mound. There were hundreds of mounds filling the canyon base! Parker secretly held her breath, prayed, and wondered how she, Henley, and Edison had been so fortunate to escape harm during the assault. She fought to maintain her composure.

Stefanos held his medallion to his beak and spoke in a tongue Parker didn't understand. Her heart thumped, and she didn't know what to expect. The pain was raw and fresh. He gathered his mourning cloak about him and raised his wings. The colossal bonfire roared and cast long, eerie shadows into the sky. The cries and chanting ceased, and he began to speak.

"We sadly say goodbye to our brothers and sisters who join our Spirits in the Sky. The Spirits have called for them. It is their time to return to the heavens high above us. May the Spirits protect them and hold them dear in eternity."

From within the great circle, every few feet along the rim, a torch was thrown into the canyon. Stefanos lifted his wings into the air as one torch after another blazed onto the pile of bodies. The fire burned and a droning silence vibrated within Parker's head. Her whole body shook. She stole a look at Henley and Edison, and they too were shaking.

Stefanos voice boomed, "Today, we come together and mourn our losses. Tomorrow we will begin our preservation of the safety and security of the Upperworld, our homeland."

His calculated words dropped like pebbles into a

lake—the water rippling long after the stones sank to the bottom. The fires burned as the canyon transformed into a glowing smolder. A flurry of hooting like screams of pain resounded and faded within a few minutes. Parker dared not breathe. Then, very slowly, a shifting pattern of movement began to circle the rim of the canyon. The cloaked forms silently rose in the air, swallowed by the night.

chapter ten

The smell of smoke still clung to the air. When Parker had last been in the Great Hall, the stage was on fire, the wispy walls disintegrating, the perches burning, and the bodies of the dead strewn about. But now, the Upperworlders had repaired the stage and most of the perches had been replaced. Even the clouds had rejoined to create the walls of mist. And the poor souls who lost their lives had been laid to rest.

Stefanos wore his mourning cloak, wrapped his talons around his perch, and positioned himself with Belliza and Vibius to one side of his wing. Stefanos caught Parker's eye and motioned she flank his other side with Edison and Henley. As the leaders arrived in a solemn procession of despair, Parker waited for questions to be asked and answers to be given.

Stefanos peeled back his hood with the tilt of his wing and revealed the eye patch had been removed. The deep red scar over his eye reminded them of how close the attack had come to hurting their leadership. "We've suffered a terrible loss, my Great Ones. None of us want to believe there could be a war here in our own world. In our castle. But we must be careful of whom we accuse. The worst possibility of all is that the Underworld is instigating our destruction."

He spoke cryptically to Vibius in their tongue. Then he turned his attention to the room. "Before this attack, many of you, including me, did not want to believe the Underworld could be responsible for tainting our water reserves on Katamoor. But now, after the brutal assault, just as we welcomed our earthlings, we are forced to scrutinize all possibilities. As of now, no one has claimed responsibility. It is unclear who executed the destruction.

"Today, we come together to put a stop to all of this. We are taking action. I have formed a task force to investigate the debris and remains from the destruction here at the Citadel, as well as at Katamoor in the areas where our water sources have been tampered. Cole is finalizing his due diligence in the Underworld. All findings will be presented as soon as our analysis is complete. I am also stepping up security at all portals. Our immediate goal is to preserve our safety and security. And if possible, protect the whole of Spyridon." He rested for a moment and studied his leaders. "Questions?"

One of the largest birds in the Great Hall, with the body the size of an elephant, covered in gray and black quills, lumbered from his place and took the lead perch.

"Great Sky King, I speak for the Titans. I have seen Cole's initial reports from the Underworld, and they do not reference any poisoning of our water sources." He stared down the Ruling Great One. "Why pick an enemy we have no proof exists?"

"I agree, Great Cranwell. Cole's reports are not worrisome. But still we must probe deeper," Stefanos said. "Without a plan for protection or purification, we will be forced to leave our own kingdom. We will be left without a single resource for clean water. It is difficult to say these words, but we will not be able to live here among our own any longer. None of us wants to believe this to be true. But we will not stop until we know our enemy. And when we do know, they will pay."

Vibius, nudged Stefanos and whispered, "If I may say a few words, Great Sky King." Stefanos affirmed and Vibius turned to address the Great Ones, "I support you, our Ruling Great One. But suggest we take action first. Now." In a gruff and hawkish tone, he added, "Without drinkable water, we are on a path of annihilation. I suggest we put together a show of force first and demonstrate we will not be anyone's victims. And then, as the Underworld is the likely culprit, we will let them prove to us they are not to be blamed."

Stefanos spoke to Vibius privately and Parker wondered if he was objecting to the aggressive stance Vibius proposed. Stefanos closed his damaged eye with an elegant movement of his wing tip and gathered his cloak around him. His prominent beak pointed to the top of the Great Hall and he appeared distracted. Parker sensed the buzzing vibration again. She recalled Stefanos wore the same odd expression when he received word that Cole was arriving. She prayed Cole would appear again. If so, it was just in time.

Moments later, all eyes turned to the entry. Cole entered, knelt before them, and looked around cautiously before addressing Stefanos. "Great Sky King, I have an urgent bid from the Underworld. The leadership requests a meeting at a neutral location. The request is for one emissary who speaks for the Sky King, and no more than five others. They promise peace. Is your permission granted?"

Stefanos tipped his beak. "Granted. If they come in good faith as you say, I will meet them off Zonoros Point. On the sand bar where we cannot be ambushed. They must arrive tomorrow at daybreak. Not a moment before."

He turned to Cranwell. "Prepare your troops for the meeting. I want your protection for our shoreline. Set up blockades a mile out to sea—they'll serve as checkpoints to stop and clear whomever or whatever attempts to pass. The falcon troops will hover overhead. We must take every precaution.

"Great Cole, tell the Empress and her brother no weapons will be permitted on the site from either side."

"Yes, Great Sky King."

"Then we shall be safe. The Spirits of the Sky will watch over us. The Underworlders will not be able to approach out of the water. I will handle their envoy on my own. If trouble arises."

Stefanos returned his focus to Belliza and Vibius, "I

have often thought the impossible. Or improbable. If the Underworld was responsible, do they have an alternate planet to which they can migrate?"

"They will have to, Great Sky King. Another war will render Spyridon uninhabitable," Vibius said.

chapter eleven

Before dawn broke, the Titans' blockade moved to its position within the specified radius of the white-capped shores surrounding Zonoros Point. Stefanos had chosen Zonoros for its expanse of shallows; any militant Underworlders would be clearly visible long before they ever became a threat.

In the middle of the night, Stefanos had requested additional protection. He ordered a trio of archosaurs, ancient and fierce feathered dinosaurs that dated back to Spyridon's earliest days, be brought to the Point, a safety measure, just in case any funny business erupted below the sea. They would remain hidden unless instructed otherwise. Troops of falcons circled above the Spyridon Sea throughout the evening, searching for movement in the waters.

At night's peak, Belliza appeared in the Sky Box, at the sleeping quarters. She awakened Edison and Henley from a deep sleep, though Parker hadn't slept a wink. The meeting with the Great Ones had given her the chills. Her mind replayed visions of sea monsters all night. Her nagging brain kept asking what these Underworlders looked like? Could they be trusted? The evidence against an Underworlder attack seemed strong. Could all of their allies be trusted?

The Upperworld delegation had begun to gather and assume their stance along the shore, a good way off. Each troop carried the Upperworld banner and stood at attention. The number of troops and their flags stretched into the distance. The line traversed the shoreline to the north and to the south. At the tip of the Point, Stefanos hovered. He would not touch down until he sighted the arrival of the Underworlders.

Parker shuddered, worried about another surprise attack. Edison and Henley stood quiet, and she thought they must be as worried as she, or just plain exhausted.

"What of the request for no more than five?" Parker muttered.

Stefanos must have picked up, either her words or her intentions, because he turned toward her. "They are well outside the perimeter I specified. Any emissary should have time to make a retreat before they arrive."

Vibius agreed. "It is merely a show of force."

"I wonder what dark things lurk below those waters," Edison said.

"I don't wonder at all. In fact, I don't want to know. Not now. Not ever. I just want this to go right. No fireworks, no explosives. I think we've had enough of that," Henley replied.

"Right, I'm with you. Talk of peace would be fine with

me," Parker added. "But if the Underworlders didn't do it, who did?"

"Hmm—we have lots of choices. The blonde dude with the wings—who knows what side he's really on? He could be full of it," Henley said.

"How about the old hawk? He's a force and pretty scary. He's ready for the kill to me," Edison said.

"You mean Vibius? Or Stefanos?"

"Yeah, take your pick," Henley said. "Could be anyone."

As the sun finally broke over the horizon, the sea water swelled and the layer of mist on the ocean burned away. The waves gathered and rushed, rising to great heights. The Upperworlders stayed put along the shore as the warm water lapped onto their feet.

Edison squeezed Parker's hand. She met his eye and noticed he held Henley's hand, too.

Fifty heads rose out of the water in unison. Heads popped up in all shapes, sizes, and colors. All with scales and most with human features. Some with hair. Some without. In the center of the group, a large red-haired man with a full rust-colored beard rose above the water to his full height. His feet remained in the water. It took some time, but eventually the man and his honor guard drew close. Only when he halted his approach did she notice a fine sheen of scales covering his body.

Stefanos dropped from the sky to meet the broad-shouldered, red-haired man eye to eye. Parker found herself staring at the strange, yet handsome man who rose from under the sea. No mistaking his strong and muscular build. And his youth. Especially in contrast with Stefanos. She thought he was probably not much older than she. Who could he be?

"We are aware of your troubles and are sorry for them," the red-haired man said. "But none of this has anything to do with us."

Stefanos still did not speak. Parker figured the Underworld had called for the meeting. Perhaps Stefanos wanted to listen to what they had to say. Unprompted.

"The Empress insisted we come to you, declare our innocence, and ask if there is anything we can do to help."

Vibius stepped forward, "Perhaps your guilty conscience brings your visit, Pantione. Or maybe you came to see the destruction for yourself."

Stefanos listened and cocked his neck toward his cousin as he touched the bronze medallion to his heart. Parker thought, could they be role-playing good cop/bad cop?

Stefanos interrupted Vibius, "If you truly come in peace, then we ask you to police your waters and portals and report any suspicious activity. Perhaps there is someone among you who wants to do us harm. We are certain this is not an interplanetary attack."

The red-haired man drew closer to Stefanos, their faces practically touching. The troops raised their arms in a defensive motion, though they held no weapons. Three massive snouts, peeked from between the shoreline and the sea, and the waters rose in every direction.

"Don't play with me, old man. You won't win. Not this time," the redhead said.

Stefanos raised and lowered his wings, signaling his troops to stand back.

"We have offered you our condolences and aid in repairing the damage from this most unfortunate event, as instructed. I have a message from the Empress." He held a folded note in his hand and extended his arm to Stefanos' talon.

Stefanos unfolded the note and read, "We wish you no harm, Ruling Great One. But if the attack on your castle was at my hand, you would have been warned and you wouldn't be standing here talking to us. You'd be with your Spirits of the Sky."

As Stefanos tucked the note into his cloak, the fifty scaly figures sank back into the sea.

chapter twelve

"We are going for a quick tour of the Upperworld, Parker. The zun beckonz uz."

Parker trailed Belliza through the air, absorbing the strange vista below. The absence of wind created a stillness and quieted her mind. The intensity of the images of the meeting at Zonoros Point, still stuck at the forefront of her thoughts.

"Belliza, I keep thinking about what happened this morning on the sand bar. Um, with the Underworld. Their leader denied having any part in the attack. Do you believe him? The leader, the one with the red hair and beard, he seemed so honest."

"We cannot be blinded by how thingz appear, Parker. We have been fooled before. We could be fooled again. Bezidez, who else would be interezted in uz? Our world, we have nothing to offer anyone except the Underworld. Perhapz they have raized an army to avenge their fallen from the war twenty yearz ago. We won't worry today about thiz now. The Sky King wantz you to zee the

Upperworld. Try to enjoy the flight, it will help free your mind and eaze your worry."

Belliza's words helped release her doubt. She breathed deeply and floated behind the tiny bird. Her shoulders relaxed and the tension evaporated from her body. Perhaps she had reached what Hungarian scientist, Mihaly Csikszentmihalyi termed the state of flow—an energized focus which triggered her complete enjoyment in this ability to fly. Belliza had explained she would instinctively understand flight and pick up the ability over time, but could it be so simple? Impossible, more likely. On the other hand, telepathy and fish men who could breathe beneath the seas were compelling arguments against the impossible.

She tried to shake off the fear of falling. After all, they hadn't let her fall to her death yet. "Belliza, where are we going?"

"There iz much for uz to do, but firzt, I want you to zee where Edizon and Henley are beginning their training. I think you will find that comforting. We go to the Kingdom of Pazzaria." Belliza hummed. "It'z a happy place, the home of the Zongbirdz."

They circled and slowly descended through the clouds and mist. When they emerged, Parker peeked below at a peculiar structure of branches and bark. Fluorescent leaves crisscrossed the tree limbs, spreading a lush brown moss between the gnarled branches. From within the bark and moss, a halo of light broke through revealing a secret city constructed of sticks and branches, yet suspended midair, just as the Sky Box and the Great Hall had been.

A melody rippled through the air. The atmosphere resounded with cheerful chirping and further relaxed Parker's mind and body.

"We'll ztop now. I want to tell you about Edizon'z training before we obzerve him. We won't dizturb him today, Parker. He needz to work and connect with hiz zkylark, Melizma. I think it bezt he doezn't zee you. He iz adapting quite well, I think."

Parker's eyes adjusted to the glowing, diffused light.

"Do you zee him below? He iz zitting bezide the zkylark—the one with the magenta throat."

Parker searched for Edison and took a double take. He stared intently at a reddish bird with a majestic purple-colored throat warbling a tune as Edison harmonized along with her. He appeared mysteriously calm, intent on creating music with the skylark. She wondered how this training would help solve the problems of the planet.

"You seem puzzled, Parker."

"Yes…no. Uh, I thought *we* had special gifts for *you*. But it looks like the skylark is teaching Edison. I thought it would be the other way around."

"It may zeem zo, and may be true now, but we are a land of many languagez. You will come to know the difference. There are callz that bring uz together to prepare for a journey or a battle. Otherz are uzed to diztract, to protect, and to warn thoze around uz if we need to ezcape. There iz even a language of friendzhip and love. Each haz a diztinct zound you will come to know and truzt. To help uz, you muzt learn about uz firzt."

"I feel spellbound by her movements, Belliza! What just happened to me? I'm feeling dizzy." Parker tightened her forehead and sharpened her vision to track the songbird and Edison before they vanished out of sight and into the dense forest of tiny homes which composed the songbird city.

Through the haze, Parker flew across the Upperworld cloudscape behind Belliza. "We zhall be in the Region of Kokobur zoon. It'z where Henley iz training. It iz quite far—almozt on the oppozite zide of our planet from the Citadel."

They journeyed through the clouds until Belliza slowed her pace. "Directly beneath uz iz Katamoor, where you went with the falconz. We'll ztop now, juzt for a moment zo I can zay my prayerz. Thiz iz the home of my family. The legendz zay thoze of uz from the land of Katamoor, the land of the Viragoz, are ztrong of heart and zpirit. I mizz my mother. And her counzel. Zhe waz a wize woman. And very dear to Ztefanoz and hiz father, Zonoroz. I only hope to be az brave and wize az zhe."

Remaining still for a fraction of a moment, she then performed a ceremonial dance just as the falcons had. As she finished, Belliza lifted her tiny foot and touched her beak to her ankle wrapped with a small band and a dangling amulet. Parker had not noticed the ornament on her ankle before, similar to the metal one Stefanos wore around his neck. Jolted, she realized this was the first time she had ever seen the hummingbird stop moving.

"I do not like to pazz by Katamoor without offering my gratitude."

"What are you wearing on your ankle, Belliza? Stefanos wears something like that around his neck. Is it the same?"

"In a way. The amulet iz from Katamoor. We believe it connectz uz to our powerz. And protectz uz when we feel weak. Now, we go on to Kokobur."

Another long, endless flight later, Belliza finally slowed as the clouds began to thin. In the vast expanse, Parker deciphered stone gray-blue promontories peeking above the clouds.

"We're almozt to Kokobur. Do you zee the tipz of the peakz—the very tall mountainz of limbz and branchez? We have another ztronghold here, a place for zafety. It'z the land of our builderz, the engineerz. It'z the home of our Weaverz. There'z no other place like thiz on Zpyridon, nor on Earth."

Belliza stopped, and Parker could tell she had more to say. "I don't want you to be afraid—it may frighten you."

"Everything is scary, Belliza."

Belliza led her through the clouds and down into the Port of Kokobur. A pungent odor rose from within the clouds and Parker covered her nostrils. Her stomach twisted and surged. The fierce smell made her eyes water. "Smells like Animal carcasses. Fowl and foul."

Belliza continued twisting and they dropped deeper below the clouds and into the surrounding wooden structures. It was hard for Parker to see a few feet in front of her. "This is pretty gloomy, Belliza. Not like the happy place where Edison is training. I hope Henley is okay here."

"Henley iz very okay. You're about to zee for yourzelf."

Suspended from the limbs of the stick formations, intricately woven, oval-shaped nests contained long tubes. Belliza cleared the branches from the nest's entry, and together they slid down through the elongated passage. Further inside the layers of sticks, Parker spotted Henley's sheath. She watched Henley, who seemed in awe of a bright green Weaver currently positioning limbs into place.

Belliza raised the tip of her wing to Parker's mouth in a motion to stay quiet and observe.

Henley started laughing. "I always thought I was good at building things. But you have it all over me. Your nests are awesome. You practically have a city here floating on a cloud. How do you get stick foundations to stay suspended in the sky? It's a miracle. Or tell me, is it magic? Cuz it defies everything I know about gravity? This is very cool!"

A shrill cackling filled the nest. Parker covered her ears.

"We zhould go now, Parker. I want to leave before it'z dark, and the Wolfbirdz come out. I'll zecure the nezt now," she said as she replaced the pass-through's twig cover.

They squeezed out of the passage and into the dank air. Belliza fastened the branches back into place. Eerie howls—a hybrid of a wolf howl and a bird trill—echoed as darkness fell. The disappearing light turned the leaves to shades of gray, and the threatening howls deepened. From behind her, a voice boomed through the mist. Parker froze in her tracks. A sharp pain jabbed her bare left foot. She wanted to cry out, but something told her she mustn't, and she remained silent despite her instincts screaming at her.

"Who are you and what are you doing here?"

Parker couldn't turn her head to see from where the voice came, but the odor suffocated her. A rush of nasty air whirled above her head. The odor blew directly into her face, paralyzing her limbs, and knocking her over as easily as if she were a blade of grass. Two rows of huge pegged and jagged teeth faced her. So large they could surely crush her bones and snap her in half.

A rope encircled her throat and squeezed tightly. The coarse twine rubbed hard against her neck, leaving her skin raw. Her neck stung with a burning, unimaginable pain. A rapid-fire puffing sound battered her ear drums. The clatter suddenly transformed into a high-pitched yipping coming directly from a double row of teeth cracked open just wide enough to reveal the cavernous jaw in front of her. Quickly, masses of gray and black feathers and rows of jagged teeth surrounded her. The hot breath attacked her from every direction.

A small trickle of light appeared on her hand. It was coming from Belliza's eyes! The rope around her neck slackened. Space wedged open a few inches and a breath of fresh air penetrated.

Belliza and the jagged-toothed creature exchanged an unintelligible, hurried communication Parker didn't understand.

Belliza whispered, "Theze are the Wolfbirdz I told you about. He iz the lead wolf, Chieftain of Kokobur. I wizh you hadn't met like thiz, but he will not harm uz now. He knowz who you are. The Wolfbirdz have been inztructed by Ztefanoz to enzure the zafety of the Weaverz and Henley. They muzt be vigilant."

The locked jaw of the hulking Chieftain began to move. Like Stefanos, another giant, he appeared about eight feet tall. "You trespass here, Parker. If you do not let us know you are coming, you may very well end up a fine appetizer. Watch your step and be careful. These nests in our domain are not very friendly."

Parker gasped and stared at the giant flying wolf. With a start, she acknowledged, and not for the first time, she was one of only three humans. Unable to fly, unable to breathe underwater, without telepathy, with no predator's instincts or capabilities. She was no warrior.

chapter thirteen

No sooner had the Citadel appeared in the distance than an obtrusive burst of bird calls startled Parker. The air vibrated. The noise, so intense, forced Parker to cover her ears. At first, she worried there might be another attack. The noise had pierced the silence with such quickness and wasn't letting up. She called out to Belliza who seemed to float with the melody as if in a trance. Waving her arm and alternating between blocking her ears, Parker finally caught the bird's attention. "What's up with that sound?"

"Ah, of courze. I zhould have warned you. It iz the chant of the Zongbirdz. The humming iz our lifeline. They chant to thank the Zpiritz of the Zky for the zuztenance from the Virago Treez. The chant happenz every week at thiz time. The zongz are prezent acrozz the planet. After the chanting, the Rock Dovez gather and diztribute food, grain and water to all of our kingdomz." Belliza's usual cheerful buzz turned a bit melancholy. "Though zeemz of late, everyone iz grumbling. The Rock Dovez have been peztering the Zky King. Our people are not happy with the water rationing. No one iz getting enough. But what can we do under the circumztancez? We are ztill blezzed to have food and water. They muzt remember what iz important! I am zo zad for Zky King, there iz much tenzion."

"Understandable. Of course, everyone is upset." Parker asked, "But I'm not familiar with the Rock Dove species? I don't think I've ever heard of them before."

Belliza smiled, "In New York City, you call them pigeonz. They are really quite elegant, though a bit cocky. They dezerve more rezpect than your city dwellerz give them. Zky King holdz them in very high ezteem, that iz why he iz diztrezzed by their reportz of the bickering in our zkiez. They, too, are an important part of our lifeline."

Parker's ears were still ringing when she reached the Sky Box, but thankfully the chanting had stopped.

When Edison and Henley caught up to her, she said in a tone as matter of fact as she could muster, "In case you were worried about those loud noises before, Belliza explained it's a weekly prayer chant. The Upperworld believes the prayers reach the Spirits who ensure their food supply flourishes. I was a little scared and thought we were being attacked. Were you?"

Edison and Henley's eyes met, then returned to her and Belliza. "Yeah, we were wondering," Edison said. "When I was in Passaria with them, they mentioned the chant and the weekly practice. Didn't think it would be so loud and spooky. Thanks for the explanation," Edison said. "But, now having asked us, where have you been?"

Parker grinned and decided to go for some humor. "Let's see. Perfecting my flying. Putting my life in danger with some birds which look more like wolves than birds. Interesting stuff. I hope your stay has been as enlightening as mine."

"So, while you've been cruising about on a joy ride, we've actually been productive and are beginning to figure stuff out," Henley snipped. "How they've adapted to live here is nothing short of miraculous. Their homes, their communities, the skills they've perfected—these Upperworlders are pretty amazing. Right, Eddie?"

"You need to come with us, Parker," he said. "I've been with the Songbirds and Henley's been with the Weavers. Believe it or not, they are teaching us to work with some of our own talents. It's pretty cool."

She glanced at Belliza and figured best not to admit she'd had a peek at their activities.

"No rezt today either," Belliza said. "Zky King azked if any of you are interezted in meeting up with the team inveztigating at the Zouth Gate. There iz a lot of damage there and before they cleanup, we are doing a thorough inzpection of the ruinz for cluez of any kind. The Great Hall haz already been through an over-haul—I did the checking by myzelf." Parker raised her eyebrows. Seemed odd, for Belliza to be a search party of one, but she didn't question.

Without hesitation, all three faces lit up and followed the hummingbird out of the Sky Box and into the wispy corridors. They floated through the Citadel clouds and

Parker wondered how anyone could find their way with the absence of markings or distinctive spaces. Only clouds thick with layers of impenetrable mist lined their path. After a while, Parker called out ahead, "Belliza, how do you know where you are in this castle? Everything appears exactly the same."

"I think on Earth you would call it a zixth zenze. We are almozt to the path that leadz to the Citadel baze, we call The Woodz. Once through the portal, the nezt openz to the Zouth Gate where we were for the funeralz of thoze lozt during the attack."

After more of the familiar jostling and somersaulting, they emerged from the jelly portal tube. Before them, twenty strong Titans and Raptors whipped through the winds of the massive stick structure.

"I have never seen anything like this. How were your Weavers able to put all of this back together so quickly?" Henley asked. She ran her fingers over the dense, immaculate wooden structure. "This foundation for the Citadel is woven so perfectly as if machinery put this together. I noticed this in Kokobur, too. And how they float in the sky is just remarkable. You must tell me, Belliza!"

Belliza regarded her. "Magic, Henley. We believe the Zpiritz have helped uz create much of what iz unexplainable."

They dove down deeper through The Woods and the canyon of clouds below it. Edison shared a solemn look with Parker and Henley, his eyes downcast. Parker empathized, it was impossible to wipe away the memories of the lit torches, the eerie procession of hooded Upperworlders. The bright white banners, pure and untouched by the debris below, still gently waved in the wind.

Belliza caught Parker staring at the flags. "Our bannerz ztay in place until we zurvey the Zouth Gate and The Woodz. We give our Zpiritz time to deliver our people to their final place in eternity."

"You grace our presence, Parker," a voice boomed from above her. Parker craned her neck upward and recognized Cranwell, the formidable Titan leader. He tipped his beak to Henley and Edison and directed, "Follow me. We are picking through the debris. You can begin here and work your way to the southwest. We covered the balance of the area, but feel free to give it another pass. We would hate to miss anything."

Cranwell turned to Belliza, "I can't bear to report to Sky King we turned nothing up. Not even a trace."

They picked through the debris and for hours worked across the canyon until the dark of night shadowed the sky. It would soon be dark. Piles of feathers and puddles of blood at every turn, but not a glimpse of anything amiss, even the tiniest fish scale, to suggest an intruder of any sort, or an Underworlder had been present.

"How will you clean all this up, Belliza?" Parker asked.

"With great care. Juzt in caze we mizzed zomething, though with thiz many eyez, I don't think we could have. Cleanup will only be difficult emotionally—you have zeen how eazy it iz for uz to move thingz around, but the feelingz, thoze cannot be put away zo eazily."

"Hmmm—I was just thinking the same," Henley said.

Edison added, "Me too. You all can do so much with the tip of a wing, or with a nod from your beaks. Have you considered the possibility an Underworlder could use telekinesis or pyrokinesis to inflict this damage? Could their powers have had a hand in this?"

"Zky King and I were queztioning that after the attack. But that would be impozzible. Only we Upperworlderz have that ability in our territory."

chapter fourteen

The tour of the Underworld loomed ahead. Parker had never been a scuba diving fan and often felt claustrophobic relying on a tank for air. "I don't get how I'm supposed to breathe underwater, Belliza."

"Your body haz already taken on the capability. Once on Zpyridon, breathing under the water will be juzt like flying for you. You didn't know you could, but you did. Naturally, or I zhould zay, magically. Once on our planet, thoze from Earth, under twenty-one develop a breathing capability which functionz like gillz. You will zoon zee."

"I recall Stefanos mentioned that. But believing it is another thing!"

"Try to be calm. I'm going to apply the Zilver Helm to your zkin. It makez you invizible to all below the zea. You'll feel zome dizcomfort, but don't be alarmed," she hurriedly whispered, "but we from the Upperworld will be able to zee each other."

A burst of pin pricks sprayed Parker's body from the top of her head to her toes.

"Ouch! This stings! Do you have to wear it, too?"

"Yez, even we muzt wear it below the zea."

"Doesn't it wash off?" She worried about the Silver Helm and the chemical effect it could have on her body.

"No, keep turning, I need to cover every inch of you."

"How does it make me invisible? This is genius. Did you birds discover this? If you did, how come the Underworlders don't know you can use it?"

"Queztionz and more queztionz, Parker! I am told it waz developed long ago by zome great thinkerz among uz, but truth be told I couldn't zay how it workz."

They journeyed downward at a blinding speed. The air pressure dropped, and Parker felt faint, but she finally equalized when they swam into a massive air bubble, a hollowed-out cave. Pierced by a shaft of narrow streaming light, the lava ceiling bore a striking array of primary colors with a stained-glass effect.

Parker asked, "How far below the sea are we? This is so beautiful."

"It'z a tiring journey, izn't it? You almozt dozed off, you zleepyhead. We're getting cloze to the beginning of the Labyrinthz of the Cavern of the Zea—the caztle of the Emprezz Diadora."

Vibrant turquoise water covered Parker's toes. "This water's so warm, Belizza. Are you sure the water won't remove the Silver Helm?" She worried about the human-like sea creatures that rose from the water at Zonoros Point. "No one will spot us, will they?"

"No, I promize, thiz water will not remove the zpray.

But there are placez where we'll have to be more careful. Not here though or anywhere we will be going to today. Zee the big arch ahead? Once we pazz through, we will be in the waterz of the Underworld."

"I'm frightened, Belliza. Stay with me."

"These next pazzagez will lead uz clozer to the Cavern of the Zea where the Underworld royalz live. Emprezz Diadora'z chamberz are in the Meridian—the layer between the Midnight Zone and the Abyzz. It'z a dangerouz path and we muzt be cautiouz. We ztill have to move through layerz of cavernz, and through The Hollowz to get there. Even experienced travelerz can loze their way. Ztay away from the rough texture of the rocky wallz, too. If you rub againzt it, you could tear through the Zilver Helm."

"How did this come to be, so far beneath the water?" Parker asked.

"Theze cavez were created by zinkholez—left behind from our fallen citiez thouzandz and thouzandz of yearz ago."

The seas continued to darken. As if turning on a flashlight, Belliza's eyes transformed into beacons of light illuminating the cave's exquisite stalactites and stalagmites. "My eyez will guide our path zo we'll be able to zee in the blacknezz of the Underworld. There are zome areaz where zchoolz of illuminated fizh are trained to light the way—it iz quite dark down here. But the Underworld creaturez have evolved and learned how to live in the darknezz."

Parker couldn't help but notice the suppressed fear in

Belliza's eyes. Not that she could pinpoint the hummingbird's thoughts, but Belliza appeared tense. Parker had learned Belliza often masked her emotions with her constant movement. Belliza must be a little uncomfortable beneath the sea even with the protection of the Helm.

"The Labyrinthz follow a circular pattern of no return. Rockz can crumble and cave. Wallz can collapze. We leave thiz part of Zpyridon to the Underworld."

Parker spotted a rock affixed with twigs and branches and stopped to pick it up.

"Put that back where you found it. You hold an ancient offering in your hand, Parker. You muzt return it. It'z a warning to be careful. Thoze before uz left the marker behind to honor thoze who pazzed thiz way before and did not return."

Parker did as instructed. Part of her wondered why a tour of such a dangerous place was necessary. "What do you mean? Not return? Did they die?"

"It is a mystery of the zeaz. They either dizappeared or were captured by the Underworld. Travel between the Upperworld and the Underworld waz frequent thouzandz of yearz ago—but it haz never been for the faint of heart. Zince the lazt war, Upperworld accezz iz limited to royalz and a few otherz."

Parker didn't want to ask, and normally wouldn't ask, but this seemed far too important. "Are you royalty, Belliza? How else would you be able to bring me here?"

"Yez, I am. My mother waz related to Zonoroz,

Ztefanoz' father. Zhe waz part of hiz Tribunal. Come let'z keep going." Belliza pointed to a narrow gap with another stone and twig marker. "The Zpiritz of the Zea wizh uz good luck. We'll go down to the final level, and then we will be at The Hollowz."

They passed through an opening in a mossy stone wall into a cloud of gas, and Parker felt as if she were floating. Fresh water, maybe condensation, must have met sea water. Last summer, at a chemistry program at the Museum of Science, she studied water purification and the properties of brackish water found in estuaries. That must've been why she felt she was experiencing a floating sensation.

The Labyrinth path morphed to a deadly black. Only the brightened flecks in Belliza's eyes cut through the smog to the saltwater caves below them. "The Hollowz are before uz, Parker. Zee the purple, iridezcent algae. It linez the lava wallz for a good ztretch," Belliza said. "You will alwayz know you have reached the final threzhold to the Caztle of the Zea when you come to The Hollowz. Everything iz black az night. Theze purple bandz of color mark the path on each zide. The Hollowz are the lazt protective barrier to the Meridian, and the Grotto, home of Commander Pantione. He iz the Commander in Chief of Diadora'z army. He iz the one who handed the note to Zky King when we met at the Point." Belliza looked at Parker and tipped her beak to proceed through the iridescent lit stone path.

"Why did we come here? I think we should turn back." She spied the bones of a small creature tangled in a bundle of dead vegetation at the bottom of the cave. She covered her eyes with her hands. Parker began to shake, and her teeth chattered. Chills ran the length of her spine. "I don't need to see this. I don't need to be here, Belliza."

"It iz important for you to know our world, our planet, *and* our enemiez. You know Cole livez here in the Underworld, watching what goez on for Ztefanoz. He wearz the Zilver Helm when he needz to move around zecretly. He too iz where he doez not belong today. He'z juzt ahead of uz, zending me zignalz, leading our way. You can't zee him yet."

"I don't want to go any farther."

Belliza wrapped her tiny talon around Parker's finger and squeezed it tightly for reassurance. "Ztefanoz ordered Cole to bring uz to the Grotto before we return to the Upperworld. We will not go to the Meridian, to Diadora'z home. Not thiz time. Do not be afraid of what you will zee. Nothing can harm you."

chapter fifteen

"This is where the Underworld leader lives? In the dark?" Parker searched the bleak space. "There's no one here. I thought Cole was meeting us."

A figure moved into the dim light. "I'm over here," a voice whispered in a subdued tone that sounded as if traveled through gasping breath. Parker then spotted the metallic sheen.

"This is the first time the Sky King has asked me to take someone from the Upperworld to the Cavern of the Sea." He may have sensed her rattled nerves, and jested, "I think our leader is testing your mettle, young lady."

"And why would that be?" She asked, quickly wishing she hadn't responded. She waited for him to elaborate. But his eyes darted to each corner of the room and he changed the subject.

"We haven't been properly introduced." He continued to tease, "The timing had been less than ideal when you arrived." Was he trying to keep her calm?

"My apologiez, Cole. Pleaze meet Parker. One of Zky King'z protégéz."

He laughed. "Aren't I his protégé, Belliza. Guess I'm easily replaced." His eyes dwelled on Parker. "This is your first look at the world beneath the Spyridon Sea. Interesting, isn't it? So peculiar in contrast to the brightness of the Upperworld, don't you think, Parker? Sometimes I wonder how the Underworlders live like this. It is often tough for me. But I've learned one can adjust to anything."

At first, Parker thought no one could adjust to a life like this. Trapped beneath the sea, in the dark. No air. No other humans. Just as quickly, her thoughts turned to herself and how she went about life in the Upperworld almost as if she belonged there. *He's right. We can adjust to anything.*

He stood closely to her and she found herself inching away. The startling blue eyes penetrated inside her, hunting her thoughts. His blonde hair swept back from his attractive face. His muscular limbs strong and capable of protecting the whole lot of them. Her nerves fired up.

"The darkness spooks me. But being under water feels natural. I think the biggest difference is the gentleness of my movements. Everything flows as you move. It's not like I expected." Ever since she crossed into the Underworld, she hadn't even considered her ability to breathe once under the water the way Belliza had described. The eeriness of her surroundings had outweighed the worry in moments.

"Glad you're comfortable. Come, we're going to the

Grotto, Pantione's quarters. I believe he is a good and fair man. It is difficult for me to accept the Underworld planned the attack on the Citadel. And, I have been on the alert, there haven't been any visible signs of involvement. Those below the sea have lived peacefully for longer than I have been here. As you know, the Underworld requested the meeting with Sky King. I am sure a clear attempt to prove their innocence."

As they moved through the darkened room, Cole said, "This is Pantione's War Room. After the attack, I expected to see documentation of the strike spread across these rocks. When there have been skirmishes between the Underworld regions, here is where strategies are planned. But this time, there was nothing."

The rock formation resembled a sizable conference table, measuring several feet high, and flattened to create a smooth surface about waist height.

"Could I have misread the attack, Belliza? There were no signs nor indication an assault was being organized. I feel responsible, but I can't change anything now, only help prepare for the future." He canvassed the area quickly and returned after a few minutes. "It's safe to continue."

Cole pulled Belliza aside, and Parker overheard him say, "She can't be more than sixteen. Who is she to Stefanos that she is privileged to come and view all of this? Other earthlings have never been down here."

Parker listened to their banter and wondered why Cole questioned Belliza about Stefanos giving her access. Her concern dwarfed his. Tall and lean, he moved with the prowess of an athlete. When he glanced in her direction, she fought to keep her composure.

In the shadow of the cave, he seemed about her age. Not much older. She thought her mother would have said he belongs on the cover of a magazine. His appearance translated as ostensibly fully human—but with his lightly feathered skin and wings, he also fit with those in the Upperworld.

"Are you safe, Cole, living in both the Underworld and the Upperworld?" Parker stammered, hoping she hadn't overstepped her boundaries.

"Yes, Parker. I am very careful. I must be."

When he said her name, a lovely tingle traveled through her body and the sensation spread within her.

"Let's pick up the pace. Pantione is having dinner with his niece and nephews. That means Diadora is going to show up shortly." Cole spoke in a hurried, brusque tone, "Let's take a look and then move on quickly before she arrives."

"Cole, explain to Parker what tranzpired between the worldz—between our leaderz," Belliza said. "Thiz will help her underztand the friction between uz."

With serious, sad eyes and a hushed voice, he said, "Following the last war, Diadora's eldest brother, Kendrick, was killed in a brutal battle at the Black Sea in the Labyrinth. Pantione and Diadora pledged they would bring up his children as their own. Their mother, Queen Ramarian, never recovered from Kendrick's death. Ramarian didn't want to live without him and poisoned herself. A solemn period in the Underworld. The battle in the Labyrinth transformed the hierarchy of the Underworld's succession. Diadora, the eldest sister, took Kendrick's role as leader, inheriting the crown. Pantione became the Commanding General of the military. As I said, he is a good leader, but a formidable adversary. He has vowed to protect the Underworld, all its people, and none with more ferocity than the ruling family. They will be next in line for succession to the throne.

"But I cannot find my way to accept they planned the strike. And, without my suspecting it? I'm privy to nearly all conversations at the highest levels of power. I am one of their soldiers, a lieutenant now, and around them every day. When could they have planned it without my knowing? Without a whisper? Who carried out his orders? The Upperworld did nothing to provoke the action. Sky King would never strike preemptively. He is a peacemaker.

"Come here Parker, before we go. There's a small opening in the rocks which will give you a glimpse at the royal family. They often enjoy a meal together. Pantione is committed to taking care of his brother's family." Cole motioned for Belliza and Parker to move closer.

Squeals of laughter flowed from within the next cave. Joyous giggles at first startled Parker, lessening the tension and lightening the mood.

Parker neared Cole and leaned into the rocky crevice to peer through the opening. His body touched hers and she absorbed the heat escaping from his skin, warming her along with the giggles of children's laughter. She breathed in his clean, fresh scent and her heart beat a little faster. As she moved toward the opening in the lava, she pinched her ankle against the jagged rock, tearing her delicate skin, piercing the Silver Helm spray and the feathered trim of her sheath.

"Hey, careful there," Cole caught her as her foot lost its grip on the moist surface. Her heart skipped a beat and she fell awkwardly into his arms.

Cole gently lifted her back into place. She stared at the magnificently carved cave transformed into an enormous dining room. Globes of iridescent coral lined the walls and cast a warm glow on the family.

"You recognize Pantione? Cole whispered. "He's the burly fellow with the green eyes and red hair. As if you can't tell. He's the only adult at the table."

"I do, but Pantione looks so different to me now. When we were at Zonoros Point, he came across harsh and rough. Now, seeing him up close like this, he seems more earthling than Underworlder." Parker didn't elaborate further but thought to herself that Pantione was physically similar to Cole in that they both had the form of a human with the exception of their skin—Cole's lightly feathered and Pantione's a luminescent texture of fine scales. Even the children could have been plucked from an elementary school on Earth. Only their skin gave them a fish-like appearance.

The red-haired man spoke through the cackle of merriment. "I am so lucky to have you, my little devils. Before we begin our dinner, I thank the Spirits of the Sea for their many blessings. May they protect you all, my niece and nephews, and the future of the Underworld. May you be so fortunate as to enjoy the whole of our wondrous planet one day. May the Spirits bless my sister, our Empress, and give her the continued wisdom to make the best decisions for our future."

Cole and Belliza exchanged glances. Cole whispered, "Enjoy the whole Spyridon?"

Belizza nodded her beak in agreement.

Cole touched Parker's shoulder, "The guards are completing their rotation and will return here shortly. We need to leave."

Cole led them through the War Room and out of the Grotto. When they reached the Labyrinth, Parker stopped to touch the stony twig marker, the Upperworld's nod to assure good luck to travelers below the sea.

A high-pitched peeping sound and a loud clacking penetrated the walls of Grotto. Bone-chilling noises shook the Labyrinth. Screaming and waves of uncontrolled sobbing filled their path. The terror followed them. Chased them. Cole and Belliza swapped glances, cueing Parker something had gone terribly wrong. More gut-wrenching screams.

"Where is the sound coming from? What's going on?" Parker asked.

"You both must leave right away," Cole said. "A problem has occurred in the Grotto. I don't think it's related to us. But best to go. I will lead the way out, but I must return to my post."

The screams beneath them finally muffled as they

ascended through the Labyrinths. They raced upward, rising from cave to cave, through the layers without hesitating before reaching the sulphur passage to the fresh water.

Belliza halted on the path. "I have zomething for you, Parker, zomething to keep you zafe and help you accomplizh all the Zky King commandz." She handed Parker a bundle which Parker carefully unwrapped. She recognized the band—it was the one with the amulet Belliza wore on her ankle. The material stretched to fit Parker's wrist and as she put it on an electric tremor ran through her. "What is this? Why are you giving it to me?"

"It haz the featherz from the owl and a root from the Virago Tree. Never take it off while you are here on Zpyridon. I want you to have itz protection." In a hushed, breathy undertone, she said, "It belonged to my mother. Ztefanoz gave it to her. He told her it would alwayz keep her zafe. And remind her of her powerz. I want you to have it. We're almozt home, Parker. We'll be back in the Upperworld zoon."

As they neared the portal, Parker stayed quiet and safe in her head. Her thoughts returned to the handsome, earnest young man who served below the sea. Then progressed to the family scene in the Grotto.

She twisted the bracelet with her fingers and said, "I can't shake the idea of this struggle between your two worlds. Belliza, is this about who rules? Kind of reminds me of the play Hamlet. Power destroys, doesn't it? And those beautiful, happy children. Stefanos, too, well…everyone seems so good. These worlds should get along." Compelled to speak further, Parker asked, "Have the children been there before, Belliza?"

"No. I have only zeen Pantione. Never the children. They are clozely guarded." Belliza reflected for a moment before speaking again. "I zuppoze I knew he had a family. I juzt never thought of him like that. To me, he iz the brother of Emprezz Diadora and the Commander of her army. Therefore, he cannot be a friend. He iz the enemy. He iz a warrior. Given the chance he will deztroy uz."

chapter sixteen

After the dizzying journey through the sea to the South Gate, and up to the Citadel, Parker flopped onto the cushiony floor of her quarters in the Sky Box. Images of the Underworld rotated through her brain as if swiping her phone—the layered caves with stalactite ceilings, the ancient stone marker warning travelers, the intricate Labyrinths. But mostly, the giggling children, the jovial Commander, and Cole dominated her thoughts. She twirled the bracelet Belliza had given her. The medallion pulsed between her fingertips.

Parker sensed someone approaching and found Stefanos beside her. He had surprised her again. "You return safely, Parker. We thank the Spirits of the Sky for guiding your journey. I wanted to speak with you before the others join us. Belliza and Cole told us there was trouble in Pantione's chambers. I am sure you have discovered we cannot account for what transpires below the sea. It is another world, far different than ours," he said. He stroked his white beard with his talon, contemplating while scanning her mind.

"Cole will be joining us later tonight and we hope he will have discovered what went on as you left the Grotto. We gather there must have been violence."

His eyes traveled back to the bracelet, as if a magnetic force drew them. Something was on his mind. She felt it from the strength of his gaze.

"I trust Cole's instincts, though. If an act of war took place in Pantione's chambers as we suspect, it had nothing to do with us."

The bracelet on her wrist throbbed. An electric charge ran through her body and vibrated in her head.

"You wear the amulet now. You have everything you need to help us protect our future." He hesitated and under his breath, he mumbled, "There is not enough time...to accomplish everything I must for Spyridon."

"What do you mean not enough time? Why?" Parker asked.

"My reign will soon be over. And it will be apparent. It will soon be time for my succession. The Spirits of the Sky will be calling for me." His eyes focused on her bracelet.

Belizza entered the Sky Box, followed by Cole, his expression grim.

Stefanos spoke in his tongue, then returned to English. "Now that Parker has seen our planet, she and the earthlings will work with each kingdom to address the toxicity in our waters. This is our first consideration. Our people are up in arms. They are not accepting the rationing and the pressure is mounting. We must come up with a solution before there is a revolt. We cannot be undermined. Once in place, we will deal with the world beneath the sea, if they are behind these crimes."

"Sky King," Cole said, "I regret having to interrupt you, sir. But my request is time-sensitive and important."

Stefanos nodded and said, "You may continue."

"You know of the incident in the Grotto. I ask for your understanding to take leave immediately. This morning, flags of mourning were mounted along the Labyrinths and continued into The Hollows. Something terrible happened while we were in the Commander's Grotto. I need to be accounted for in the Underworld. I can't be missing. If this is some kind of crisis, I want to see with my own eyes what happened. I will transmit my findings at the first opportunity."

Parker held her breath, hoping Stefanos would release him. She did not know the rules of this land, nor the hierarchy of their roles, but she had the impression no harm could come from him. He made her feel safe. Even if he was one of them, she trusted him.

"May I take my leave, Sky King?" Cole requested.

Was she imagining Cole stealing a quick glance at her before he vanished? She felt a hint of something between them.

Belizza spoke to Stefanos in the tongue of Spyridon. Stefanos tipped his beak in consent. "Go forth, Cole. May the Spirits of the Sky be with you and guarantee your safe return." He waited until Cole left and turned to Parker.

"Now you have gained a better understanding of our world. I want you, Henley and Edison to join the team investigating Katamoor. I think you will also find your inspiration there for purifying our water. Leave the world beneath the sea and the political ramifications to us."

chapter seventeen

With the grim message of Stefanos nearing the end of his reign, worry swallowed her up. She worried for herself, Edison, Henley, and all those on Spyridon who were the beneficiaries of his strength and leadership. She debated how much to reveal to Henley and Edison when they returned to the Sky Box. It was another in a series of concerns, both about the near future and possibly their ability to get back to Earth whenever the time came. However, they had a world to save, and this news would only distract them from the task they'd barely started. They'd already had too much of that. So, for now, she would keep it to herself.

"So, I think we've seen enough of this planet to begin our work on solving the water crisis. We are due to go to Katamoor. We need to do our own site check and determine if we can pick up anything. Maybe it's hard to see for the Upperworlders—you know the expression, the forest from the trees. Maybe we'll bring a different perspective."

"After traveling the regions and learning about their

ecosystem, the Viragos are definitely Mangroves, but far from ordinary ones." Edison said. "The species is pretty impressive. Scientists on our planet understand the benefits of the Mangrove ecology. On Earth, Mangroves are harnessed to act as natural filtration systems—shifting sediments, desalinating, and improving water quality. So, if we find out how to correct the toxicity where the Virago Trees are through filtration, we should solve the problem. And those Viragos are more than what you could call super-charged. Whether it's magic or some natural aspect we can't figure out—those trees are feeding the whole Upperworld and providing every single necessary resource. Hard to believe, huh?"

Parker nodded. "We don't have the sorts of tools we need to provide the answers to those questions...and it doesn't matter, as we get results."

"So, filtering the toxins through the Virago Trees could be our answer?" Henley asked.

"We'll need to find which materials work best for the filtration, how much we'll need, and come up with an engineering and design plan. It's got to be kinda simple, based on what we have to work with here. Am I being too much of a nerd?" Parker asked.

Henley laughed. "Yeah, you are. But a nerd is called for now."

Edison half-smiled. "Makes sense for me to help locate materials we can tie back to the Virago Trees. I've been through the regions, and for sure the Upperworlders know where the best resources are and how to find and transport them," Edison said.

"Yep, you probably are the only one to get everyone to collaborate anyway. Everyone likes you," Parker teased. "And you have your smooth hum of a voice that wins everyone over."

"And my father always said I had to be an engineer." Henley said, "Guess I should be the one to work on the design/build phase. If he could only see me now! I spent most of my time with the Weavers," Henley said. "Must have been on purpose. Damn how Stefanos knew it. I can try my best. And logically, the Mangrove concept should work. But can we rely on conventional, um, Earth logic here?"

"We'll have to rely on our knowledge," Parker replied. "And trust our brains will lead us to the correct solution. We have to believe in ourselves. OK, I'm a nerd again. I'll track all the details and work through the scientific principles. Science lab was always my favorite place to be. Do we agree we have a plan?"

"Yep—we have a plan!" Edison said. "And as much as we can control it, we have to be flexible because we all know things can go wrong." He was right: a science experiment was just as the word implied— an experiment. You did all the hard work, hoped your analysis was right, and you hadn't miscalculated. But if one little thing was off, everything vanished in a second and your heart was in your stomach because your experiment flopped.

"Parker? Henley? Let's make a pact, a pact we won't let anything stop us or distract us. We're going to keep going until we have a solution and it's in place."

"If we get a curveball, we duck and immediately stand up and start thinking fast how to correct it. Got it?" Edison asked.

Edison extended his right hand, the one bearing his ring, and Parker and Henley followed, layering their hands, followed by fist-bumping. The bracelet pulsed on Parker's arm. A current of electricity ran through Parker, from top to bottom, sealing their promise.

Spirits at work, Parker hoped. "Tomorrow we return to Katamoor and go to work."

chapter eighteen

Parker fiddled with the bracelet, still questioning the logic that an inanimate object could keep her safe. The idea of an amulet protecting her contradicted everything she held as truth. While in the Underworld though, she'd vowed to wear it until she returned home.

The sky lightened as Parker neared Katamoor and she realized she had overslept. Now she'd be late to meet up with Edison and Henley. The falcons circled in the sky above her, tracking her movements. The Virago Trees buzzed around her as if speaking, trying to tell her something.

She spotted Henley and Edison in the distance at their rendezvous point. Both wore knee-high boots, fashioned out of rubbery bark. Smart. She looked down at her own bare feet as the muddy ground squished between her toes and wished she had put on the boots that had been left in their quarters, the sinking, porous feeling giving her the creeps.

High above, their falcon bodyguards circled and kept

vigil over Katamoor. A few agents perched on the roots of the Virago trees, shifting uncomfortably and ruffling their feathers. Parker didn't blame them for the discomfort; Holy land, shmoly land—not for willy nilly footsteps.

Edison and Henley, deep in conversation, kept in step making their way through the tangle of growth and wild vegetation. For a brief instant, Parker felt like the outsider again, but pushed the thought away. As she neared, Henley had stopped and stood with one hand on her hip while she gestured with the other. Her words traveled above the quiet bog as Parker approached.

"Just when I began to think I was okay with her. She pulls this crap—a no-show. I'm just about done with her, Edison," Henley snapped. "That high and mighty attitude... I bet she thinks what she's doing is more important than what we're doing." She snorted.

"Henley. Cut her some slack. You and I have been together a lot. She's the one who's alone. Who knows what they have her doing? Let's give her some more time to show up. We all have our responsibilities, and none of us will get anything done without the others. When she says she is going to do something, I believe she will take care of it. I just hope nothing's wrong."

"I am concerned, Eddie. What if we can't solve this? My whole life just about turned around and this happens! I need to go home—I never thought I'd be wishing for that."

"What, to go home?"

"Yeah. I felt like I was getting on track. I don't know

why I ever agreed to stay."

"What do you mean—on track?"

"You know, trying to learn to play guitar and sing in a band. Not play the violin like my parents wanted in the school orchestra. So, I went to a pawn shop and bought my guitar for fifty-six bucks with my babysitting money. I planned on becoming the local girl who made it big. Whether my parents approved or not.

"Mostly I wanted to tune out my mother and her nagging. I changed my name to Henley in middle school." She twirled her hair. "Most of the other Chinese American girls at school had already changed their names. But my mom says, 'Your father and I chose to name you Ming Mei because you were the smartest and most beautiful baby.' Or, 'Why aren't you proud of your heritage?' I would tell her we're not in China. We're in America. If you wanted to be Chinese, why did you move here?"

Silence reigned for a spell. Henley's intensity had rooted Parker to the spot, and the terrain hadn't helped to get her to move either. She'd almost pulled a foot free of the sucking mud when Edison spoke up.

"I know. I get it." he said. "No one ever understood why I didn't want to be a jock." He flexed his muscle and teased, "I had the build for it. Not that you can tell any more, I think I've lost my bulk on this bird diet," he joked. "But I just wanted to be in the Detroit Choir. But I had to listen to my folks with the whole med school thing and how I should be a doctor. God gave me the gift of smarts— I should use it. But I kept thinking, my voice is a gift, too.

I guess none of it matters now."

"Don't say that! The last thing I remember, I'm wearing a black leather mini dress with cool, outrageous feathers and a pair of black nylon boots with super high heels." She smirked, "Feathers. I should have known!

"I looked the part though and Cory, the manager of the band I wanted to join, didn't even care if I could play guitar. I think he thought I'd look good on stage. Figures, that's how most of you guys think! Then I started playing, rapping into the mic, and the jerk comes over and tries to full-on kiss me. I push him away and tell him to back off. The band starts laughing. He didn't like that—me taking him down in front of them. I go to leave, and he follows me out the door, and can you believe it, he tries to kiss me again."

"Did you want to kiss him back?"

"Yeah. He was hot. I wanted to, but I needed to be on an equal playing field with him, just like the guys in the band. Then we're both outside. Alone. And I tease him and say, 'So I'm in, aren't I?' He gives me a snippy look and says, 'Pixie, don't ever presume anything with me. Do you think you made the cut?'

"I say, 'Of course I did!' Calling me Pixie. Now I'm pissed. He's testy but laughing, 'Someone's cocky. Just like me.' But then he tells me I'm in."

"You had to be happy then." Edison guessed.

"I was, Eddie. But it gets better. He says to me, 'You're cute. I'm thinking about kissing you again, but you told me to back off.' I tell him, 'I don't like surprises.'

"He says, 'I'll remember that.' I ask him if he likes surprises and he said he does, but it depends. So, I kiss him really hard on the mouth. And take off. Now I'm the one in control! Boys! Why does it constantly have to be about you guys?"

He laughed hard. "Trust me, we guys don't feel in charge. Not by a long shot!"

Henley cocked her head and asked Edison, "Aren't you worried about what your folks are thinking?"

"Yeah. I keep wondering—did they go to the police? I think I feel the worst for Ozzie. My brother. He's supposed to be looking out for me. He probably feels it's his fault. That he's responsible because he didn't wait for me so we could walk home together."

"I pray we can help them, and that nothing goes wrong," Henley said. "The sooner the better, you know. I want them to have clean water, right, but...I got my own problems."

Edison began humming. He softly sang the tune of the Spirits of the Sky—the one Melizma had taught him, the one that assured their protection from the evils below the sea.

Henley glanced over at Edison, she stopped pacing, and walked over to stand beside him.

"Ok, let's give Parker some more time," Edison said. "We can go over what we've put together again. She'll be here soon. I'm sure of it."

Parker edged closer, still unobtrusively. Edison and Henley hadn't taken notice of her approach. Her bare feet hadn't made any noise in the mud. Parker didn't want to interrupt their dialogue. She knew their conversation hadn't been meant for her. But she hoped her time to share feelings with them would come.

At that moment, Henley did an about-face and peered directly into Parker's eyes.

"Sorry I'm a little late," Parker called. "I actually slept a few hours. Miracle of miracles."

They seemed happy to see her and Parker felt a little guilty having eavesdropped. She said, "Well, what do you think about this spot? Can we make it work?" A sense of adventure replaced their earlier expressions.

Edison put on a ghostly imitation, and said, "Only if the spirits say so. Are you listening, spirits?"

Henley jumped in with him, "If there is a God, he'd better be listening, or I will bring out my mom's chant—that'll scare the spirits." With her next step, Henley's boot sunk to her knee in mud, entwined in a knot of black muck.

"My boot won't budge!"

"Don't taunt those spirits, Henley," Parker said. "See what they can do?"

"Whoa! I can't move my right leg!" Henley wrestled to free her boot from the tangle, her words choppy, as she pulled on her thigh.

She managed to yank her foot out of the muddy boot and turned to Edison again. "Can you please come over here and help me get my boot out of this mess? I am *not* walking through this place barefoot. I'll leave that to Parker."

Edison pulled on her boot, struggling with an invisible

force that seemed to retaliate. Each time he pulled on Henley's boot, it sunk deeper into the mud. "What the heck? I feel something is pulling your boot down on the other end!"

"What? No way! That's ridiculous. Give it a yank. I'm not walking outta here without it!"

"I'm trying." Edison's face was covered in sweat. "Henley, if I can't pull it out, I'll carry you. One more time. Let's try together."

"Let me help." Parker said. "Maybe the three of us can manage to move it. Could it be some form of suction? The pressure of an air pocket you stepped on?"

All of a sudden, the boot popped out with ease, as if the Virago Tree had wanted them to recognize its strength.

Henley stepped back and said, "Now that's weird. How did that happen?"

Edison scratched his head and went on, "I'm thinking maybe we shouldn't be here. You know this is a special place for the Upperworld."

"Now you sound like Parker. You don't believe that, do you?"

"I don't want to. But I wonder if there's a message here. Why else would the boot release? Maybe the Spirits don't want us to mess with them. No rational idea is gonna make sense to us anyway."

"Now you think a tree can think. A tree has an ego. Parker, let's not go there," Henley said. "Please."

"I don't know what to think. But let's be respectful of the sacred nature of Katamoor and the Virago Trees. We can't go wrong with that philosophy." As she spoke, the bracelet pulsed on her wrist.

"These trees have my respect." Edison said. "Let's keep going with the plan." He smiled. "Let's have it, Parker. How do you see this working?"

"Mostly, I think we have to look at this like a science project. I believe Stefanos knew Katamoor would provide the answers to us. That's why he guided us here."

"Hold on, Henley," said Edison. "As bizarre as this place is, if Spyridon was once like Earth, parallels should exist. Go ahead, Parker."

"Let's say the Virago Trees have the benefits of the mangrove ecosystem that they do on Earth. Based on that, our solution might be to be to find a material that will act as a membrane—a porous netting that will trap the toxins as the water passes through—in a way, replicating nature. It should work, even here on Spyridon. It'll need to be supported by the tree's root structure, though, so it doesn't collapse.

"Henley, you're the engineer so you'll need to figure out a plan to strengthen the root structure. The only roots here though are the Virago Trees, so we'll need to extend or expand that base to build on, or the filter won't hold."

Parker fingered the bracelet as she spoke and wondered if it sent her the answers.

"I get the root structure," Henley said. "but I'm no chemist. And I don't want to be or need to be. Let's keep going and leave that part up to Edison."

"It's pretty simple," Edison answered. "Something like

an aquaporin from the protein family. Something that is capable of transporting liquids. You know what I'm talking about, Parker. Maybe you do too, Henley. The discovery of Aquaporin actually won a Nobel Prize way back in the early 2000's for its synthesis ability in water channels. Aquaporin netting will trap toxins, and the active ingredient will purify the waters in the Upperworld."

"There is something else I just thought of. Might be an interesting benefit. Edison, do you think it's possible that we may be able to lessen or prevent soil erosion and even reclaim more land for the Upperworld?" Parker asked.

Edison chuckled ruefully. "Might be possible, but again who knows what will work here? We aren't playing with the same rules."

"My part sounds simple enough," Henley said. "Edison, yours is challenging."

"We'll get there once we locate the materials, and they'll need to be plentiful to pull this off."

Henley looked off into the distance. "Check this out..." She pointed toward a Mangrove that appeared somewhat separated from the others. A host of Pigeons, or Rock Doves rather, had congregated around one of the Virago trees chattering to one another.

"Hey, you know what they call Pigeons here? It's funny, but it fits when you think about it. Belliza told me." Parker smiled and said, "Rock Doves. They're the purveyors of the food and water. Maybe they're gathering resources. Stefanos said there's a lot of rumbling about the water rationing. None of the Upperworlders are satisfied. I guess they are worried that there won't be enough water to keep them alive."

"I get that. Let's go over there and see what's happening," Edison said.

Getting there ended up being a long slog; the regular mud went even thicker, until a sort of marshy pond opened up before them. Suddenly they found themselves wading up to their knees in muddy water. Above the water, buzzed clouds of annoying, teensy insects. The water deepened until Henley and Eddie were forced to keep to the edge, or have it overflow and fill up their boots. Parker was up to her waist in the murky water.

Henley spent most of the time swearing under her breath. The whole ordeal took a good fifteen minutes, and by the end of it, Parker wished she could fly without Belliza or Stefanos around.

The birds took off as soon as they neared the tree.

"Strange," Henley said, "Pigeons, er, pardon me, Rock Doves, are never afraid of anything. Especially people."

"Maybe, like everything else, they're different here," Henley said. "Let's check out what's going on at the tree. Look—seems like a natural spring bubbling up." At the base of the tree, a patch of stones washed up with clear water which flowed out into the basin they'd just been through.

Edison overturned one of the rocks with the tip of his boot. He bent over to pick up what looked like a bunch of gray muddy feathers.

"What are you looking for?" Henley asked.

"Not sure, I just noticed one of the Rock Doves

picking around this stone. Thought it might be something more interesting, but turns out they're just some dirty feathers, probably nothing. But for precaution, I'll take them back with us. The birds were so close to this water source, and it appears to be clean, fresh water. Makes sense for us to check it out."

Parker said, "Yeah, let's take some water samples, too. If this water is as clean as it looks, maybe the Rock Doves found another water source. Do we have anything we can carry it in so we can take it back with us?"

"What kind of scientists would we be if we didn't?" Edison said as he pulled a bunch of small vials fashioned from leaves from his pack.

Henley stared at Parker's bracelet as if seeing it for the first time. "Where did you get that? One of the Weavers described a bracelet like that. She said it had special powers. I don't want to scare you, but I wouldn't wear it. If those spirits can get us stuck in the mud, what can they do when you wear a bracelet which doesn't belong to you?"

Spontaneously, Edison hummed, then softly began to sing:

Put me upon the feathered stem, for I have the power to help.

The night is mine. I wake when others sleep.

I can see in the darkness and discern coming danger.

We must be able to care for each other.

The warrior must be alert and ready to protect against prowlers in the dark.

I have the power to help so that there will be no danger

during sleep.

I have the power to help and be watchful against enemies while darkness prevails.

I have the power to perform these ceremonies in the night as well as the day.

"Where did that come from?" Parker asked. "Edison. Edison!"

Edison's eyes glossed over, looking at her, but through her. Then, he just glanced up at the sky and Parker began to think he was ignoring her.

She repeated, "Edison! Can you hear me?"

"Yeah. But I feel funny. What did I do? What happened?"

"The song you were singing—it sounded like beautiful poetry."

"I-I don't know. Parker. Something came over me. The words came from me, inside me. But they aren't mine. I sound nuts, don't I? What is this planet doing to me?"

"You aren't crazy. We're in a world we couldn't dream up. And right now, we are in the most spiritual spot on this planet. No wonder we are feeling something. Henley, do you feel anything different?"

"I'm feeling pretty scared just listening to you two." Henley said, "Maybe these trees are wishing we would go away and leave them alone."

"Well, that's not happening." Parker said. "But we have our work cut out for us. Between the Upperworld and the Underworld, there's enough strange stuff happening, I think we can safely say there is magic everywhere."

"Parker, speaking of the Underworld, why haven't you told us what you saw down there?" Henley said. "Are you sworn to secrecy or something?"

Encouraged by Henley's effort to communicate, Parker weighed the risk of telling them about the terror and the beauty of the world beneath the sea. They all needed to know what faced them.

Parker explained her ordeal under the sea, with Henley constantly interrupting with questions she was about to answer. This included the Silver Helm, the pleasant feeling of weightlessness, the strange way she could breathe beneath the water, the glowing fish, and most importantly the mysterious incident with Pantione, the Underworld general and father figure.

"...I'm watching this family of fish people all sitting at the table, laughing, and having fun. I want to say it felt normal, the way they related to each other. They were like people, and not bad people, either. It made me think that everyone should be able to get along, like this environment should work for everybody, in both worlds."

Edison listened intently and nodded in agreement. "You know, Parker, if our plan works—and I believe it will, maybe it will promote a better peace."

"You're right, and we know living organisms need light to survive. What if our project not only purifies water for the Upperworld but also somehow provides light for those below the Spyridon Sea? The darkness is oppressive down there."

Parker didn't mention what happened as she left the

Underworld—the screams, the terror. Remembering her mother's words—you need to know when to stop speaking before you say too much. Because then you will lose everything you've gained.

"I am going back to the Citadel," Parker said. "I want to talk to Belliza about our idea. Let's regroup back here tomorrow—same time."

Parker stepped with a new lightness. She had to admit how good it felt to be part of something. Maybe she was finally being accepted.

She walked away, listening to their chatter, reflecting on her own thoughts when something yanked her foot downward. She pulled on her foot, but the swampy mud wouldn't release her, just like what had happened to Henley. But the swamp began to pull her down. She dropped knee-deep into the murky ground and the gravitational force wouldn't release and drew her lower and lower. The mud covered her body, slowly reaching her neck. She opened her mouth to call out for help. The words disappeared. Blackness surrounded her. A swooshing movement rushed from above, and a brush of wet, sticky feathers attempted to lift her out from the depths of the sludge.

Her falcon bodyguard appeared overhead and said, "Parker, grab my talon!"

The wet swampy ground plugged her nostrils and sucked her down. Eyes closed, she searched for his talon. She panicked. She covered her nose with her free arm and attempted to pull herself up. But the pressure dragging her down was too forceful.

Stefanos' voice came through muffled and distant. "Parker! Parker!" He repeated her name again and again. "No! No! You can't be taken from us. Not now! She mustn't go to the Underworld. She cannot be there alone!"

Parker's body yanked in two directions, as taut as a rubber band about to snap. The last she heard was Stefanos say, "I pledge to you, Parker, you will return to the Upperworld."

The sloppy blackness consumed her swiftly.

chapter nineteen

When the mud cleared, Parker opened her eyes and peered beneath her. Two razor-thin strips of neon light, one blinding white and the other sapphire blue, guided her on a downward path. She plunged into a whirlpool of motion. The neon stripes, speeding ahead of her, paved a lit path through the blackness. The spiraling descent slowed to a less furious pace, and Parker was keenly aware she had entered the Underworld. Had she fallen into a sinkhole? Or had someone or something pulled her down? She steeled herself with the knowledge she had survived the Underworld before.

The smell of sulphur rushed at her. She was nearing the entry of the first Labyrinth. The reflecting light of the glowing stripes illuminated the lava walls and cast a purple haze through The Hollows. She tried to block the memory of the Grotto along with the blood-curdling cries, Belliza hustling her to keep moving, and Cole desperate to return them to the Upperworld. She shivered as goose bumps broke out along the length of her arms.

The two neon stripes stopped moving. She swallowed and gasped as she took in the physical form of the creatures sporting the glowing neon. She blinked back the image of two miniature seahorses with human heads and torsos, and curling spiked tails staring back at her. They could be a male and a female, or even both. Their torsos glimmered—one in rich garnet with a stark white neon glow and the other black striped in blue neon. The black one had a heavy beard matching closely cropped hair while the garnet one's hair curled in a flowing mane of blondeness. If she hadn't been so frightened, she would think her abductors were beautiful and friendly. But friendship was not on her mind. And she couldn't presume to read their inscrutable expressions either.

Parker wondered if they would converse with her in English. She opened her mouth to speak to the creatures, but loud voices distracted her. Shocked into recognition—she was certain one of the voices belonged to Cole! Had he come to save her? She remained hopeful and quiet, realizing she must not call attention to her familiarity with Cole, and compromise him. Had he seen her? She wasn't wearing the Silver Helm. If he had, he did not acknowledge her presence.

An assortment of eight huge creatures—some with human features, others with crustacean parts, wore all black and guarded the path outside The Hollows. Each held a dark navy flag with a circular golden crest of a fish curled in on its own tail.

A voice from under the helmet of one of the guards

called out, "Don't move, Lieutenant. You've broken the Empress's rule. Why aren't you wearing the proper uniform? We are in mourning. We have orders."

A shackle whipped from behind Cole and encircled his left foot, then his right, locking him to the spot. The guards exchanged glances but did not speak.

Cole held his head high. "I've been assigned other duties."

He must have been afraid, but he refused to show fear. Cole's voice grew louder. He thrust his shoulders back and raised his chin. He stood up to the guards, though they towered over him by at least a foot. Cole ordered, "Now, remove these locks from my feet and let me pass." He held his stance and snapped. "The Empress is waiting for my report."

One of the guards motioned toward a room beyond, where Parker could make out a few more guards standing over one of those map tables for making war. The group exchanged words with the guard, then one of them left and returned within minutes with another sea creature, one that was more sea creature than human. The creature edged sideways like a crab, across the floor of the Labyrinth. Its human head sat on top of a wide, long, hard shell with four pairs of legs thrusting forward from underneath the shell. Each of its legs wore a similar shell-like armor. The two front legs were finished with jagged claws.

"We meet again, Scavenger," Cole spit out the words, saliva landing on top of the creature's shell. Cole glared. Parker thought she detected a smirk. The Scavenger must have earned his moniker from the odd sweeping movement with which he scuttled about the caves. He looked like a hunter about to trap whatever stood in his way. His claws appeared sharp enough to shred metal. Parker thought he could easily make a meal out of an errant soldier as well as decaying seaweed.

"What have we here?" The Scavenger removed a sword from his belt. He poked the point into Cole's belly. With a quick flick of his claw, he slashed open Cole's jacket, tearing his vest, and tracing a thin line down Cole's chest with the tip.

Parker winced as the steel edge opened Cole's jacket and revealed the light dusting of golden feathers. Blood trickled down his skin and onto his vest.

Cole held firm.

"I recognize you, Lieutenant Sky Man. How dare you disregard Her Highness's orders? What makes you think you are above the law, especially today of all days? We are in mourning."

Still Cole refused to budge.

"Get the foragers! Take him to the Tank," the Scavenger directed the sentries. "Let's see what the Empress wants to do with him."

The neon blue-striped seahorse whispered to the one with white stripes. "Let them pass. I don't know what the Scavenger is up to, but let's stay out of his way." The white striped one said, "He's up to something. As usual. But this one is our responsibility. After they pass, we'll take her to the holding cell."

Parker shivered in the shadows. Her hands tied, and her voice paralyzed, her body freezing. Her gaze drifted along the dark passageways. Flags with golden symbols hung from the lava walls lit by the purple haze. There appeared to be hundreds of them, hanging limply like tree limbs damaged during a storm—heavy and weeping in sorrow. The guards had said the Underworld was in mourning. Were these flags of death? There hadn't been any flags on this path when she had been here with Belliza. What had happened?

Her eyes darted about the Labyrinth. The murky path had appeared beautiful to her with the companionship of Belliza. Now, with the seahorses, she was struck with a sense of cold, sullen silence and pure isolation in her humanity.

Disturbed by the encounter between the Scavenger and Cole, she feared what might be ahead for her. Her heart sank and her body caved as despair threatened. Her lips quivered and her limbs shook uncontrollably. She had never felt so alone and unprotected. She touched the bracelet to her cheek. An electric charge surged and whipped through her, shocking her body from slack to erect. An inner calm locked in her brain and signaled strength. She would need it to survive.

chapter twenty

"Toss her in," a grumbling guard directed the seahorses. This one was more human in shape, but his skin was covered in the deep gray armor of a lobster, and the spines of an urchin sprouted from his head and ran down his back. He pointed to an open rusty metal door and said, "I'm not touching her." The seahorses took her by the arms and hauled her into the cell. She crashed against the stone and winced in pain as she hit the mossy wall.

"Take off those ridiculous feathers and put on the prisoner's uniform of the Underworld." The guard skulked in the shadows and threw a pair of roughhewn dark green pants and a short-sleeved top at her, and said, "You've earned the right to wear it. No feathers dare show themselves here."

Dull eyes, absent of color, sat square in the middle of the guard's flat face. Parker figured his scaly gray skin had never seen a glimmer of daylight. Prominent gills puffed in and out as the guard's chest rose and fell in a lazy manner.

She hadn't noticed gills on any others in the Underworld. Yet. But then again, she was breathing in the Underworld without gills and flying in the Upperworld without wings. Go figure.

"You won't be wearing clothes for long any way. You'll be dead before you know it. We'll probably burn ya naked. The birds boil pretty easily down here."

Parker trembled. Fire? Tears started to form in her eyes. What were they going to do to her? More importantly, why?

Grateful for the shadows, Parker cringed as she undressed and breathed in the worst odor she had smelled in her entire life—closest to the rancid smell of the corpse flower at the Brooklyn Botanical Gardens. The putrid odor soaked the air of the small cell. Barely a fraction of light, only murky gloom, seeped beneath the crack at the bottom of her locked door. Slimy lizards scampered across the floor but kept their distance. She prayed snakes wouldn't show up. She never liked handling them in lab, or even at the zoo, let alone this miserable hole.

The guard took a quick pass at the bracelet Parker wore on her wrist and backed away. She instinctively covered her arm. "Please sir, may I keep it?" she asked.

He didn't bother to stifle his laughter. "Sure, as long as you don't hang yourself with it. Come to think of it, hanging yourself might be preferable to facing the Empress." He wise cracked loudly as two more guards passed by.

"She could end up like Veto," one of the guards joked.

"But I doubt they'd leave her to watch the Black Sea where she'd be gobbled up in one bite. Nah, don't think she'll be so lucky."

"No, she'll not be as lucky as Veto. After all, he just lost his arms and his tongue. They say it was Stefanos who silenced him and cut it out. Our Empress wants everyone to have a voice—howling and whimpering during the torture."

"The Spirits of the Sky won't find you here anyway. And even if they could, they wouldn't save a murderess like you. Commander Pantione would be understandable, but what kind of monster kills children? Nope, you'll have something special waiting for you at the end of your trial, something the likes of this planet has never witnessed."

Murder! The last Parker had seen of the Commander and his family in his quarters, they were alive and well. But then, she had heard the screaming. Parker had no reason to kill anyone on this planet—or any planet! What kind of demon was the Empress? Stefanos had said little of the Underworld rulers. He hadn't even determined if they were responsible for the attack on the Citadel, and there'd been no evidence of their involvement either.

The guard wadded phlegm in his mouth and spewed it into Parker's eyes. "Empress Diadora will gladly watch you suffer. Maybe you'll be dropped into our bottomless pit, and you'll be devoured in teeny-tiny pieces." With an uproarious laugh, he goaded, "The birds will never find you."

"I didn't kill anyone!" She doubled over from the

roiling nausea brewing in her belly. She tried to find bravery within her but collapsed in a heap. Without food or sleep, her strength faltered.

At first, she couldn't tell day from night. But after, she studied the minute details of the shadows beneath the door and began to notice the nuances. The first hint of glow. The imperceptible lightening of the black to gray. And, back to the blackest black. She drifted off and slipped into the cool darkness, her head aching and bruised.

Spring bloomed in Central Park. She meandered around the reservoir with her parents, a typical Saturday. Her mother had packed a picnic lunch and spread a blanket on the grass for them. Parker wandered over to the flowers to watch the bees moving among the fresh, young buds. A hummingbird circled nearby, then grazed her arm. Her mother called out, "Parker, how lovely! Hummingbirds don't usually come into contact with us. They keep their distance. This one likes you." Her mother had smiled, her eyes sparkled. Parker returned her mother's gaze and glanced back at the small bird. But it had disappeared. She woke with a start. She hadn't thought about that incident for so long. In her dream-like state, the tiny bird wore the triangular black mark and the amulet on its foot.

Time passed. Possibly days until footsteps sounded, moving toward her cell. A brisk clicking hit the subterranean stone. A jiggle of a key wrestled in the lock. Parker rose, and losing her balance, she grasped the wall for support. The door opened. A fantastical, magical woman in a shimmering emerald gown loomed over her. The woman's skin gleamed with light shimmer of tiny scales blazing a red so bright, Parker's eyes hurt. A luxurious, neon-red braid of thick hair wrapped the woman's head several times. Green luminous eyes, like daggers, ripped inside Parker's chest, chilling her bones, and making her skin crawl.

Parker gasped. And the woman hadn't even spoken a word. Her imposing presence filled Parker's cell—a ten-foot-tall wonder of a woman. Curvaceous, and more human than fish, with the exception of the fine scales. The Amazon stole her breath. She had never seen anything more beautiful or more frightening.

The Empress cast her gaze back to the guards, nodding to those who lurked behind her. "Leave us. I wish to be alone with this one. The murderess of my brother and my successors. She will have my undivided attention."

The guards disappeared, and the Amazon stepped into the cell, slamming the door behind her. In the shadowy darkness, the reddish glow, the only light, beamed from the core of the Amazon.

"You wretched earthling. Tell me *why!* Why have you done this?"

Escape was the only way out of this! Parker covered the bracelet with the palm of her hand, willing it to give her the courage to speak to this beautiful demon.

She summoned a breath to form clear words. "I have no idea why you are accusing me of this crime. A terrible mistake has been made. I've done nothing. There is no reason for you to believe I committed murder. I would never hurt anyone." She rubbed the bracelet with each breath and her spirit toughened. She knew the Amazon wanted to bring her to tears, to break her down, and demand she be fearful.

The woman flamed a deeper red and her body glowed as if on fire. The Amazon pointed her index finger at Parker, and suddenly, Parker's face burned hot. The skin on her hands smoldered, searing pain shot through her. She fell onto the cold wet floor. Her skin blistered as she burst into sobs, writhing in agony like a child.

"How does that feel? This is just the beginning." The Amazon laughed. Her cruel eyes revealed a sick pleasure in witnessing the fear written on Parker's face. "I am Empress Diadora, Queen of the Underworld, and I am not pleased to meet you. My pleasure will come soon enough, though, when I torture you within an inch of your life. And I promise, you will wish you were dead."

She stepped in closer, breathing heavily. As she swished around Parker, the full-body burning sensation returned. Parker screamed and rolled against the moss-covered wall as her pants began to sizzle and fry.

"You are Parker—the earthling Stefanos has brought to save his people. I suppose *he* sent you down here to do the miserable deed for him. He's a pigeon-heart, afraid to take me on, so he sends a helpless waif like you! And he calls you his protégé. Rather amusing—a fool such as yourself! What can you possibly do without powers, without any prowess? I am quite surprised he thinks a child like you could help him at all. Why, you can't even help yourself."

She laughed for a brief moment. And the sound rippled through her cell.

"How sad, you won't have a chance to help the Upperworld, anyway. You'll be a distant memory." She called for the guard, and the door opened. She turned, spun back around, and sauntered over to Parker.

"Oh, and I forgot to tell you, you *will* be prepared for trial, Parker—by week's end. You'll be charged with the murders of my family. My court will judge you before the Spirits of the Sea, and I can tell you now, you will be convicted. You will pay dearly for this crime. Everyone in the Underworld will bear witness to your slow and painful punishment."

"I had nothing to do with your brother's murder or anyone else in your family!" Parker moaned. "I only saw Pantione once—when he was enjoying a meal with young children."

"That's right, Parker. You were there. We've placed you at the scene, and we know the poison you brought with you comes from the Upperworld." She called out to the guards, "I hope you overheard her confession. Come in, Hercala and Orion." The two neon-striped seahorses appeared at the door to her cell. "Our earthling has just admitted her guilt. Add her acknowledgement to our trial preparation."

Fighting tears, Parker managed a hardened expression. "I'm guilty of nothing. You misjudge me. Your accusations belong elsewhere. Not with me!"

A flash of fire ripped from within the Empress and

singed Parker's arms. The door to the cell closed. Blackness again. Diadora's angry footsteps trailed off, echoing until the sound disappeared.

Darkness smothered her. The black quiet settled in her cell. The pain of burning echoed and came on fresh again. The cool floor and walls brought no lasting comfort; her skin continued to relive the fire again and again. How had the Empress brought fire to her hands? And the torture Diadora described terrified her more than the idea her life could be over.

She wiped her tears away with the back of her hand. The amulet's jagged edge scratched her tender cheek. Electricity raged through her. Her swollen eyes followed a path in her mind. Multiple dark passages situated a level or two beneath her cell. Each hollowed out, and quite narrow. The Labyrinths of the Underworld. Her brain pictured them clearly, curling and curving, as though she were walking them with Belliza or Cole. Though the meandering path appeared to go nowhere, one of the paths must lead to the portal to the Upperworld.

Parker blinked wide open and released the vision imprinted on her brain. She knew what she must do. Her eyes fixated on the darkest corner. She stumbled and fell to her hands and knees. The amulet guided her brain and vibrated the closer she moved to the spot she had pictured in her head. She would dig her way to safety—to the hidden portal and on to the Upperworld.

chapter twenty-one

Buried alive. Parker's body prickled with pain. Her raw, blistered skin sparked at every touch. Her temperature raged, swinging between hot and clammy to chilled and frozen. She worried infection would set in if her burns weren't treated soon.

She pushed past the agony and chipped away chunks of the rocky floor. When footsteps approached, Parker rolled onto her back, concealing her tunnel. From outside her cell, soft, subdued voices bantered, but she couldn't distinguish the words. She stopped digging. She hadn't heard voices since the Empress had disappeared. Could she be in shock and imagining things?

Words Parker didn't understand interrupted the heavy silence. Then a loud snapping. Curling and snarling sounds came from the Labyrinth path or maybe from another cell next to hers. Lashings? The snapping paced consistently as if measured by a metronome. No moaning or groaning followed the cracking.

"Ready to admit the truth yet? You scumbag. You try

to live among us, and you stab us in the back and show no respect. I, for one, never believed you! Bring on the truth before you die," the Scavenger said. His voice remained unforgettable.

Who was he talking to? Could it be Cole? She prayed not.

"Try as you like. You can't hurt me, Captain."

Cole! His voice weak. Almost unrecognizable.

Could they have discovered Cole's connection to the Upperworld? After all these years had he been exposed now?

The staccato clip of heels pounding on the stone penetrated Parker's cell. The unmistakable voice of the Empress. "Enough Captain! Leave him to me."

"So, it is true. I didn't believe the Scavenger. You have dishonored me, Cole, by ignoring my call for mourning. Of all my soldiers, I would not have thought this of you. You disgrace the memories of my family. How dare you? Not just Pantione—but Kendrick's offspring—my heirs to the crown. My entire Kingdom." Her voice drifted. "I regret honoring you with the lieutenancy. I granted you this recognition, despite all my captains having little liking for you. They think you are still one of them. But Pantione and I... Well, we believed in you."

"I did nothing, Your Highness, except serve you with respect," Cole said. "I went to the Upperworld for a reason. I needed to see what I could learn for you. To find out if the poisonings in the Grotto were retribution for the attack on the Citadel and the water poisonings in the

Upperworld. And, I have news you will want to hear."

"I want nothing from the Upperworld! Not even the intelligence you gathered from spying on your estranged Sky King. I don't need confirmation—I am certain! Have you forgotten where you reside, which side you are now on?"

Parker listened closely.

"I am your ruler now! Your commands come from *me*! Who sent you on this mission to the Upperworld? How dare you plan your own strategy? Especially while we mourn. Now is the time to honor my beloved family. Later we will get to the bottom of this. And then will I deal with you."

The metal door slammed with a bang. Keys rattled in the lock.

Parker returned to her tunnel. She worked through the blackness into more blackness, following the pulse of the amulet. Time passed, and it was nearly impossible to judge exactly how much. A day? Maybe. Her fingers went raw from the digging, but she gained a measure of comfort when grasping the amulet.

She had made progress but stopped again when the sharp clicking of heels returned. The sound of keys banged against the metal door next to hers and must have opened Cole's cell.

"And so? I am curious, what is this news I must know?" the Empress said. "Poison is clearly how the faint of heart would wage war. It is what your Sky King would do, not the likes of us who know no fear. Perhaps you should be eyeing your own. Besides, poisoning may not bring about a quick death. In fact, sometimes it may not work at all." The Empress stopped, and appeared to have caught herself, Parker thought. What did she mean poisoning didn't always work?

"Your Highness, something unusual is happening. We need to know who is behind it. I undertook this mission for *you*, Your Highness. I am not confirming or denying Stefanos struck out at Pantione. Perhaps he did, and if he did, I will find out for you and he will pay. But we cannot attribute Pantione's murder to the Upperworld just yet. What *is* true is the Upperworld is pointing its finger at you for the thousands of deaths across their kingdoms.

"I ask for clearance to return to the Upperworld. I can find out what they are planning. I know how to move around them. I will bring you back the truth. I am the only one who can do it." Cole's words came through her wall rational and calm. He continued, "You know Stefanos embraced me, Empress. Almost like a son. But I am not of his people." A strong argument Parker thought considering all that had transpired.

"And then, I came to you. And you and Pantione accepted me and let me into your world. To serve. And serve you I have, faithfully."

Diadora laughed deeply. "They will all perish, and it cannot be soon enough for me. You fail to mention the earthlings. Do you think I am stupid? I know Stefanos is behind this treachery. These earthlings arrive and I am to believe this has nothing to do with me or my people? And days later, my family is poisoned! I have judged them, and now I will judge you."

The metal door clanged shut. Parker wished Cole knew she was on the other side of the wall, but she dared not make a noise.

The guards continued to bring her food and water twice a day—algae, seaweed, fish eggs—not in the least bit appetizing, but enough to sustain her. Each time they approached, she lay flat and concealed the opening to her tunnel. She sensed the guards staring at her, despising her, but they did not come near.

As she scraped through the rock, she replayed the conversation between Cole and the Empress. Cole knew she had no connection to Pantione's death, but he couldn't provide the alibi. And the toxic waters in the Upperworld? Diadora denied it adamantly, along with the assault on the Citadel. If those acts of war were at her hand, she would have declared her intentions or at the least taken credit for the strike.

Parker had her own questions about Cole. Was it possible to trust a spy? She wanted to, very much. His beauty and sincerity had imprinted themselves on her, but now she wondered: could he be a double agent, or playing both sides against each other for his own benefit?

A shuffling and sliding of heavy feet scrubbed across the floor of Cole's cell.

"Where are you taking me?" Parker heard Cole ask.

"To the lower pools in the Cavern to wash you up, Sky Man. Empress Diadora wants you clean, not that I see why she would. You're a filthy commoner and a lowlife who shouldn't even be counted among us. You belong in the Upperworld, with your birds! But we do as Her Highness bids, so rid the blood from your useless body, because *I'm* not touching you. She'll be down here shortly. There'll be time for us to carve you up later."

With her ear to the mossy wall, Parker fought back a sob and prayed for his safety. Would they bring him back?

The Scavenger's voice reverberated through the Labyrinth. "Bring him something to cover himself. I can't look at him any longer. Though the sight of your naked self would give the Empress a hearty laugh, Sky Man. She could use one. Ready him—the Empress is on her way."

"And if you're thinking about any funny business, go ahead. Be foolhardy, because then I will get to have some fun should you decide to cause trouble. Nothing would make me happier than slicing off an ear, a hand, or a foot perhaps. Better still, clip your wings! Just watch your step!"

The loud clicking of heels on stone returned. The Empress called out to the Scavenger. "Thank you, Captain. I can handle this conversation on my own. I will call you if I need you. Open the door and take your leave."

"I believe your story, Lieutenant." The Empress said. "Tell me more. Let me untie your hands."

Why had the Empress changed her tone? Parker hung on every word. Could she be trusted or was she baiting Cole? The Empress had berated him, accused him of siding with the Upperworld. Now her voice had turned sweet and soft, purring like a kitten.

"Empress, please. I know you are distraught," Cole

said. "Many things are unclear."

"Not any longer. I've learned exactly who committed the crimes. The earthling they call Parker. I will crucify her, and everyone in my kingdom will bear witness. She will suffer like no one ever has."

Parker's body quaked with each voiced accusation.

"Your Highness, none of the earthlings could find their way to the Grotto, let alone move about freely."

Parker dug her nails into her palms. Would Diadora believe him?

"I have evidence. In fact, my Wizards of the Sea, Hercula and Orion have abducted her. She is here in the Labyrinth as we speak."

Parker's heart pounded in her chest. What evidence could Diadora have found?

"I'm not sure I understand," Cole said. "What are you talking about, Empress?" The clicking of Diadora's heels moved about the cell.

"Open it."

"A feather? So?"

"I know the provenance of this feather is from the Upperworld. It is a remnant from the gown of the earthling, Parker. From her tunic." Her shrill voice now overtook her earlier calm. "A gift from Stefanos, I presume."

The metal door scraped open. The Scavenger must have entered Cole's cell. "Your Highness, is everything okay? Shall I remove him now?"

"No! I told you I will call you when I need you,

Captain," she snarled. "Go away!"

"The feather was discovered in the War Room, next to the service area of Pantione's dining room," Diadora said. "Clearly, the earthling did this. The feather proves her guilt. She must pay. Even if Stefanos planned this, she will be crucified. I will see to it personally. Besides, I am hopeful we will soon have corroboration."

More movement in the cell. A delicate sigh and then the rustling of fabric. A deep breath and a longer sigh. Were they touching?

"The earthling wasn't entirely successful. My clever brother has spent years working up his tolerance to a number of poisons. We are optimistic he will be saved. He is not yet speaking, nor is he quite alert, but he will be. And we will soon learn the truth.

"Kendrick's children, though. My niece and nephews..." The Empress broke off into sobs. "They will never take their rightful place in my kingdom. They are gone."

"Call the guards for some nectar, Diadora." Cole said. "The juices from the sea garden will help heal your soul."

"Thank you, Lieutenant, you're right. The nectar will help. I am joyful my brother may not be lost."

"Scavenger! Come!" The door creaked open. "Bring me some nectar from the Meridian wells. NOW!" The door closed. "Thank you, Cole. I feel a little better already."

"I know how difficult this must be, Your Highness." He spoke tenderly, and Parker hated the jealousy bubbling within her. Worse, she hated the idea she might have feelings for a traitor.

More rustling of fabric and deep sighs.

"You have no idea. I have lost almost everyone who means something to me. Thank the Spirits of the Sea, Pantione may have been spared. The rest—they are gone. Gone from the world. Gone from Spyridon forever! I will never lay my eyes on them again!" The Empress began to sob.

With her ear glued to the wall, she listened for sounds to understand what Cole might be doing to comfort the overwrought Amazon. She stopped herself from imagining an embrace.

What was wrong with her?

"But I do understand, Empress. You know I came here a young child. An orphan. I have been alone on Spyridon since I arrived. To this very day, I have no idea who my family is. No one is more alone than me. Even you have your loyal followers. Those who will do anything for you. Including me."

"You heart is pure, Cole. You must return to the Upperworld and find the truth before our whole world falls apart."

Parker's ear hugged the wall. She questioned for the first time why would Cole ever have chosen to remain on this planet? If he had been able to return to Earth as Stefanos had said, why would he have stayed?

chapter twenty-two

The evening shadows fell longer that night. The air grew colder and Parker shivered. Her blistered hands, sore from endless hours of digging, tightened their grasp on the amulet and worked through the pain. The Empress had promised her trial would begin at week's end. She needed to escape before then.

The jittery grumbling of the guards grew hushed and less obtrusive. Even the stillness in Cole's vacated cell became quieter. Still, she continued to dig through layers of the floor beneath her. At one point, she thought she perceived a humming sound, like rain falling in a distant forest. Could she be hearing things? People had been known to lose their minds in solitary confinement. Was she losing hers?

The guards stopped talking altogether. Sometimes they quieted down during what she thought of as the middle of the night.

A light melody buzzed in the background. Her mind fantasized the hum, playing tricks on her. The soft rattle of keys. Were they coming to get her and take her to trial? She steeled herself and thought, not now! She was too close to finding the path to the Labyrinth.

A key turned in the lock to her cell and Parker rolled into position. She braced herself, preparing for whatever demon would appear on the other side of the door. The metal door creaked open. The humming became louder.

Though the humming was familiar, she saw no one enter the blackness of her cell. She felt a finger tenderly placed on her lips, indicating she remain quiet. It must have been Edison and Henley wearing the Silver Helm!

Parker groaned with pain and relief.

The prickly sensation covered her from nowhere, crawling across her skin, like thousands of insect bites in every crevice. At last, the Silver Helm covered her, and the invisible swam into focus.

Cole stood before her, covered in the glittering silver sheen of the Helm. At first, she thought she was delusional from the lack of food, lack of sleep, lack of light. She dreamed of a rescue. And now, Cole stood before her. She started to rise to her feet, but her legs collapsed, too weak to support her. He lifted her in his arms. The warmth of his breath on her neck. He held her close and she felt the beating of his heart. Her body fell into the tenderness of his soft, gentle touch.

Edison and Henley stood behind him—also protected by the Silver Helm.

The door inched closed. Cole turned the key in the lock while Edison continued to hum his mesmerizing tune.

Parker mustered a weak smile and attempted to stand again but crumbled, unable to gather the energy. Her hair knotted, her hands caked with dirt, her body covered with welts. She blinked repeatedly and struggled to speak through cracked, trembling lips.

Cole motioned again to keep silent. Parker rolled slowly onto her side, pointing to the deep hole in the corner of the floor where her body had been.

"What have you done?" Cole whispered and smiled in admiration. "You are remarkable, Parker, and in the face of this danger. I see what the Sky King sees in you."

Parker pointed to the amulet on her bracelet, muddy but still intact.

Cole stared at the amulet. "When did you get the amulet?" Cole asked. "It belongs to Belliza."

"She gave it to me when we left the Underworld and told me not to take it off. It would keep me safe." Parker's voice rasped as she spoke. "I guess it has. At least so far. The amulet keeps pulsing and signals me where to dig."

"So now I know why you're a filthy mess." His words came across light-hearted, but his expression grave. "How did you know you'd be able to connect to another path in the Labyrinth?"

Parker breathed heavily, gasping for air, pushing out the words one at a time. "I didn't. But the guards were talking. They said Diadora wanted a private path to take me to trial. But then she changed her mind and decided on a public display. Somehow, I felt there had to be another way out." She spoke slowly, her breath short and her words clipped. "The amulet brought me to this spot. Maybe I was dreaming, but I figured this had to be the way. I know they want me to die."

Cole gripped her shoulders, "Don't think about that now." He held her close and her body filled with warmth. His arms enfolded her and she cast her eyes at the welts and bruises everywhere on his skin.

"You don't look so great yourself," Parker said. "I heard what you went through at the hand of the scary crab. I was listening through the walls. It's as dangerous for you here as it is for me."

"For all of us." He motioned to Edison and Henley to come close. "No matter what you see, no matter what happens—Edison continue humming until we seal Parker's cell door behind us. The skylarks taught you how to change your volume and enhance tones. Use what you learned. You will keep the guards asleep for as long as you carry the tune. Henley—let's get going on the digging," he said, pulling blades from his pack.

Edison continued to hum but not without blowing Parker a kiss.

Henley pushed past Edison and ran to Parker's side to hug her. "Oh my god! I thought I'd never be with you again." Henley whispered. "You brat —look what you've put us through! But, damn, I can't believe how relieved I am we're together again."

"Enough of the love fest, girls" Cole said. "We have work to do and we must move quickly. In less than an hour, the guards rotate. We can't let the next shift show up and find sleeping sentries."

He handed a knife to Henley and one to Parker as he removed his blade from the cover on his belt. "Do you have the strength to dig? I brought several knives. This blade will work much faster than your hands. We need to go NOW." He nodded to Edison, "Increase your volume. Once we're in the tunnel, it'll be difficult for the sound to carry. We'll have to hustle when that happens. Best for you to stay guard here and keep the volume just as it is until I come back for you. I promise, no longer than ten minutes."

Cole surveyed Parker's efforts and said, "You left the easy part for me. We're less than five, maybe eight feet from the next path which will be a bit trickier. It meets up with the public Labyrinth for maybe thirty feet. The Empress planned to use that open path to lead you to trial. From there, we'll just be a short distance from the Black Sea, right before the East Gate portal to the Upperworld. Not too far."

He sighed heavily. "The Spirits of the Sky have been watching you. They directed you to this shortened route. We only have a small window before the next shift arrives. Hopefully, we'll have passed the open Labyrinth by then. "

Cole's knife hacked away furiously at the dirt and stones.

They crawled on their bellies, each whittling away with a blade. The path was jagged and fraught with spiked formations which scratched their skin as they passed. Parker's blisters burst, but she ignored the hurt and clung to the thought they were on their way to safety.

"I'm going back to get Edison now. Keep digging. When you get to the large boulder in the path, wait for me. We'll detour to the left and after we pass, I'll reposition it to block the guards from following us. At least momentarily." He hesitated before speaking, then added, "If I'm not back here in five minutes, go without me."

Parker shot him a terrified glance.

"I'll be back. Don't even think about it."

Parker held her breath for several minutes. At last, the humming echo traveled through the tunnel. Cole and Edison rejoined them. More digging and clawing through another several feet of the path until the large boulder blocked the trail.

"My bracelet is pulsing again, Cole," Parker said. "This must be the way. We can't stop."

"Can't we dig around this?" Edison pushed his hand into the narrow crevice between the dirt and the stone.

"Ouch!" He winced in pain as he tried to pull back his hand. "Something just bit me."

There was a subtle but steady hiss. "My hand is numb!" Edison cried out. With his free hand, he grabbed his stomach and began to vomit.

Cole and Parker exchanged glances. Henley looked as if she would pass out.

"I haven't run into any snakes down here," Parker said. "I worried about them when I was in my cell, but mostly I just saw lizards, and they didn't have much to do with me. They came crawling out when I began to dig the path. I kept thinking the guard would put two and two together and figure out I was digging, but no one noticed."

Edison's breathing labored. His arm remained stuck in the crevice and he turned pale as if he would faint.

"There are snake-like reptiles in these Labyrinths," Cole said. "They burrow into the paths and strike when they feel threatened. I'm afraid they can be poisonous."

Henley cried. "How much more of this can go wrong?"

"We'll be okay, Henley," Cole said. "We need to stay calm." He put the back of his hand on Edison's perspiring forehead and rubbed his shoulder. "You're hot. Try to relax. If you were bitten by a snake and you become anxious, the venom travels more quickly. Take a few good, deep, long breaths now."

Edison nodded and closed his eyes, inhaling and exhaling slowly. Edison softly sang and repeated the verse, "*We have the power to help*," which evolved into a low, steady hum.

"We have to clear another few feet so we can cross the Labyrinth. Then, we'll be upon the Black Sea—the final path to the East Gate."

"But Edison is trapped. We have to free him and keep moving." Parker said, her brow creased. Cole wasn't telling her everything, but she nodded in agreement.

"We can't dig beyond the boulder," Henley stated. "It's serving as a support structure and holding up the ceiling along the path. If we attempt to move it, I'm sure the path will collapse and come crashing down."

"I think she's right, Cole," Parker said as she studied the ceiling. "The bracelet is telling me the same thing. It keeps pulsing. The closer I stand to Edison, the more powerful the bracelet's vibrations. I think it's trying to show us the way. We should continue straight ahead around the boulder."

"*I'm* showing you the way!" Henley said. "Forget the bracelet nonsense, Parker. I've studied engineering. I know what's happening here. Straight ahead is the only way out. I figure we can carve out a foot or so to the left of the boulder, we can squeeze through. We'll have to test as we open the wall to make sure it won't cave in on us."

Henley poked Parker in the ribs, "The prison diet has helped you, Parker. And since the rest of us have only been eating glorified trail mix since we got here, I think we'll be able to squeeze through." She pointed at Cole, "But the six-pack here, he might have to flex his muscles and suck in to fit through. Follow me."

"No body parts in that crevice," Cole warned. "Just the blades first, then you can go. There could be more of those lizards. Although they'll probably back off now, as they've sent us their message."

At a foot in, the ceiling began to shake and crumble. The moist, rocky pebbles showered their heads spraying their hair and eyes with dust and dirt. The walls began to crumble and collapse.

"No more digging! We squeeze the rest of the way through. One good thing—behind us the path will be blocked, and the guards will be trapped." Cole yelled as he ripped the sleeve on his jacket to tie a tourniquet around Edison's hand to stop the venom from traveling.

Edison's eyes rolled back. He writhed in pain and passed out.

"Please don't let him die!" Henley wailed. "He's not dead, is he? Help him!"

Cole took another blade from his pack and said, "Look away. I need to clean the wound and withdraw the poison. This'll be quick, but it won't be pretty. Don't worry, Edison won't feel a thing. He's lost the sensation in his hand, and we can't let the poison travel. We have no choice."

Cole skinned the surface of Edison's finger and the blood oozed. The swollen finger reddened. Parker watched as Cole put his lips to the wound and furiously sucked the flesh to withdraw the poison. After a few seconds, he spit out the bloody venom and tore his other sleeve from his jacket. He wrapped Edison's bloody hand tightly.

"I'm going to wake him up—the pain will have lessened. We are close now to the open path of the Labyrinth. Anyone can pass by. But with any luck—it's the middle of the night and the shift change is still a good twenty or thirty minutes away."

Cole slapped Edison on the cheek, and the boy's eyes flared open. "Sorry for the wake-up call, buddy, but I need you to help us. Use your left hand to dig. I dealt with your snake bite, so you'll be okay."

They picked their way carefully through the last rocky ledges of the cave and reached the public crossing beneath the Cavern of the Sea. Parker took in the rows and rows of flags. "They put up more flags, Cole. Why?"

"They were placed to mark the path to your trial."

Parker felt faint and stumbled. Henley rushed to her side and looped Parker's arm over her shoulder for support. She took Parker's hand in hers. "What do the flags mean?" Henley asked.

"The Underworlders are in mourning. This path marks a death sentence and leads to the cell where Parker was held. We cannot concern ourselves with that now. There will never be a trial. Eyes straight ahead and keep moving. We have to cross the Labyrinth and get to the Black Sea. We're almost there. Keep your eyes open and your mouths shut."

Edison called from behind, "Cole. Can we stop? I can barely take another step."

They paused to rest on a large rock beside a curving waterway. Two twenty-foot long, silver slithering eels glided along the surface of the gloomy water, tracking the presence of the intruders, brushing up against the boulder. Their large snouts poked into view, flashing rows of sharp teeth.

Henley opened her mouth to scream, and Edison threw his hand over her lips before the sound could escape. The eels slid back into the water. The guard had taunted Parker with tales of these electric eels. She didn't repeat to Edison and Henley she'd been told these eels were flesh-eaters that would first strike by paralyzing the body, then finish by tearing it apart, limb by limb.

"We are not out of trouble yet," Cole said. "We are almost to the caves by the Black Sea. We have to move through fast. It's our last hurdle."

They neared the perilous waters. "Edison is very weak," Parker said. "The current here is too strong. He won't be able to swim with his injured arm."

"No, I can do it," Edison said. "I'm pretty sure I can make it."

"Not a chance. I'm going to help you." Cole lifted Edison in his arms and dove into the waters. He swam against the force of the current to the other side. Parker gasped as she watched the Silver Helm wash from their bodies. Another path led into more blackness. From within the blackness a massive snout peeked out of the water. The entirety of the Black Sea moved as a gigantic sea monster rose from the waters and headed for Cole.

Cole turned back and yelled, "Jump in. Time is running out. NOW!" Parker and Henley froze and stared at the monster unable to move.

"Jump now and keep your eyes straight ahead or he'll perceive you as the aggressor. Look away unless you want to be his dinner!" Parker and Henley held hands and leapt into the water, dashing across the top of the dark rushing waters with a fast crawl. From behind a rock, an Underworld sentry stood in full sight. His jacket sleeves hung limply at his sides. No arms.

Cole motioned to the sentry, "Step aside!" He pulled a sharp blade from his belt and said, "Or I'll slice off your tongue. Answer me! Or would you prefer to die right here, right now?"

"Wait," Parker tugged on his arm. "I've heard of him,

Cole. He's the one they call Veto. The guards say Diadora punished him. He was demoted to protect the caves of the Black Sea. The guards blamed Stefanos for Veto losing speech. Some say Stefanos cursed him and froze his voice. Others said his tongue was cut out in battle. Let's leave him be. There's nothing he can say, anyway."

They had crossed the blackened waters, leaving the danger behind. They were safe.

chapter twenty-three

Henley stopped in her tracks and sat down. "My legs are numb. I literally can't take another step. If we're out of danger, can we stop and rest?" Parker flopped down beside her on the lava rocks. Their bodies leaned against a ledge which began to jostle and fall apart. As the wall split, Henley and Parker dropped backward and rolled several feet down a steep but rather shallow ravine.

"Cole!" Parker called out above her as she stood up and brushed off the dirt. "Hey! Where are you guys? We need help. We're not going to be able to pull ourselves out."

Edison peered over the side of the rocks, where the ledge had been. He stepped back quickly. His face etched with panic, he turned to Cole, "What is all of this?"

Parker revolved on her heels and surveyed the scene stretching out behind them.

Another layer of Spyridon! An entire middle world—between the Upperworld and the Underworld. Was this even possible, or were her eyes creating some kind of mirage? A massive, desolate metropolis, like a deserted movie set of destroyed, war-torn cities—one after another—extending far into the distance beyond her sightline.

As she stared at Henley, Parker repeated over and over again, "I can't believe this! All the burned-out buildings. Could have been offices, apartments, shops, warehouses, even manufacturing plants!" Her hands shook and she inhaled sharply, but still she couldn't calm down. "Henley, doesn't this look like what was once a major city? A city like New York! It goes on forever!

Parker stopped moving. "How can this be here on Spyridon? In a world with just clouds and seas? An entire city? There's not an undeveloped parcel of land anywhere. Only buildings and crumbled roadways. Bridges. Highways. Skyscrapers. Everything is abandoned. No sign of life. It's like what I think of Earth, post a nuclear war."

"Yeah, like those movies where some big city has been destroyed. Usually, decimated by an alien force. You know what I mean, like some horror sci-fi thing. Could aliens have done this?"

"Maybe it is the way Stefanos described life here, thousands and thousands of years ago. Human life did exist. If this is real, then it could only have been designed and created by humans. Birds and fish don't live like this."

Parker yelled up to Cole and Edison, "Hey guys. Where are you?"

Above them, Cole removed a rope from his pack. He tossed it down to Parker and Henley.

"Take hold of this," Cole yelled. "One of you at a time. Tie it around your waist. I'll haul you up. No messing around. We must go!"

"But Cole," Parker pleaded. "Tell us what happened here?"

"No time now. Or we may never get out."

"Cole's right, Parker. There's a rumbling of voices behind us." Henley warned, her ear cocked to one side. "Not too far away."

"Move it," Cole yelled. "You don't want to see the fury that will unleash if they catch up with us. Say your goodbyes to the Underworld."

chapter twenty-four

P arker absorbed the brilliant blue sky and welcomed the vision of the Citadel, peeking out high above her in the clouds. Cole had moved ahead and told them to take their time. Parker figured he was giving them a chance to talk amongst themselves.

"I don't even know where to start, Henley. Edison," Parker said. She brushed away the moisture welling in her eyes with the back of her hand. "How can I ever thank you?" Tears rolled down her cheeks, meandering through her scattered freckles. "You risked your lives for me. I'd probably be dead now. No one ever thought about me before, really. Besides my parents."

She could have elaborated on her gratitude, but the old Parker told her don't act like a loser with these new friends. She wanted to gush, tell them she had never experienced friendship like this—not just someone being a pretend friend to get help on a test, or answers for Bio. Parker took Henley's hands in hers, hoping she wouldn't pull away. Then, she drew Edison in close too. "You probably can't tell because I'm crying, but these are tears of happiness. I swear."

"Are you kidding me, Parker?" Henley said. "I think I was out of my mind most of the time. If I stopped to think about what we were doing, all three of us would have been goners."

"I'm just so happy you are alive and here with us," Henley said. "We're back together." Henley held her arms out to Parker and returned the embrace.

"Truth is we had no choice," Edison said. "The blonde dude made us come with him. Trust me, when Cole told us you were kidnapped and held prisoner, do you think we really wanted to go and find you?"

"I don't believe that," Parker said. On second thought, how would she have felt if one of them was prisoned below the sea. And for murder. Would she have wanted to take her chances and put her life in danger? The idea rattled in her head and she reminded herself never put herself in anyone's shoes because you never know how you will react given the circumstances.

"Edison was keener on saving you than me." Henley smirked. "I flat out said, 'No way! I am not going there.'" Henley pointed her finger at Edison and said, "But he made me do it. I wouldn't have gone if Cole asked."

"Yes, you would have, Henley. You know damn well we are all alive now because of him," Edison said.

"I know, but after I heard the word 'murder', I tuned out and started chanting my mother's Chinese prayers. I think I'm still in shock. But we both said, what's gonna happen to Parker?"

Henley and Edison stared at one another while Parker's eyes flitted back and forth between her two companions. "I think I'll be replaying the nightmare in the Underworld for years to come. Maybe for the rest of my life." She had to come back to the present. Too close a call to her mortality.

"And which horrible nightmare would that be? By my count, there were quite a few. None of them I choose to remember—but I probably will," Henley said.

"Me too."

"Me three." Edison piped in, "Though Stefanos says when we go home, we won't remember anything. Do you still believe him?"

Parker turned back to Edison. "I don't know what to believe any more. But I believe in us." She averted her eyes to his hand. "Hey, how are you feeling, Edison? I'm so sorry you had to go through this. Are you in a lot of pain? It's my fault."

He glanced quickly at his bandaged finger before he returned her gaze and said, "My ring is gone. How will I ever get another one?" And then he mumbled, "If I ever get home again."

Parker realized he had been wearing the ring on the hand with the injured finger—the hand trapped in between the crevice. He must have lost it during the incident with the lizard. She could see he fought to control his feelings. He began to hum. They may have been spared death, but as she looked at each of her friends, she knew they would never be the same.

chapter twenty-five

Up ahead, Cole kept a brisk pace despite the last twenty-four grueling hours. He approached the gate to the Citadel, stopped, knelt to clean and wrap his knives, and then returned them to his pack. He appeared confident and assured, though Parker thought his actions said otherwise. He must have been itching to get going as he rose to his feet as soon as she neared with Edison and Henley.

Cole flung his pack over his shoulder, "I can't delay my return. I have to be accounted for among the captains and lieutenants. At some point, the Empress will notice I am missing." He quipped, "If she hasn't already. Hercala and Orion could already be scouring the Labyrinths searching for me." He turned to leave and with a few great strides had already moved far into the distance. He raised his wings and began to soar.

"Hold up a second," Parker dashed behind him, "How can you go back? Please, Cole, don't leave. It can't be safe for you there. Not now."

Cole stopped in mid-air and circled down beside her. "No, Parker, this balancing act between the Upperworld and the Underworld has been my life. I have to go back."

"But, why?" Could she convince him to remain in the Upperworld? She hurt as if a knife had stabbed her soul. The rational part of her knew she had reason not to trust him, but the deeper part needed him near.

"I walk the tightrope—it is my duty to help this planet thrive. Or there will be no Spyridon. You know what is happening on Earth. You have seen for yourself how your resources are diminishing. Your shorelines shrinking. We are thousands of years ahead of you. Now, if we cannot control all we have fought to preserve, we will reach the end.

"I can't explain why I care about this world and its people. I just don't think about myself anymore..." Cole placed his hand on her shoulder and added, "...and what I might want. Tempting though it may be." His words, soft and soothing, filled her with a warm glow, but his movements read anxious and strained. Could he have been just in a hurry to go?

"Then, let me say thank you. I would still be down there if it not for you."

"You are very brave, Parker. I knew you had it in you, but during some of those moments, I was a little worried about the outcome, for all of us. Even myself. And your friends, well, they were remarkable, too. Friends, right?"

"Don't tease me. Yes, we are friends." She turned up a corner of her mouth in a semi-grin and turned serious. "I didn't feel brave though, Cole. I confronted my fear. But still, you pulled me through and rescued me."

"You didn't give up. Now you know, bravery is within you." He rubbed her shoulder and his gentle touch stirred her emotions. He caught her off guard when he stepped closer and placed both of his hands softly on her cheeks and pulled her towards him. He sought her eyes. "I've never met anyone quite like you, Parker."

His words swept her in, and the tingling sensation returned and traveled through her body. She wondered if this was what it feels like when you like someone, and they feel the same. How many times had she envied the girls at school, walking along the halls, hand in hand with their boyfriends?

Parker wanted his lips to touch hers. She had never been in such close contact with a boy. Her skin on fire, she felt as if she would explode with desire. She didn't want him to move away. Yet the nagging doubt popped back into her head, questioning his allegiance. She fought off the doubts, but thought back to the sounds emanating from the Tank: the rustle of fabric, the heavy breathing, the sighs and whispers.

What else could have been going on between the Empress and Cole? Had he manipulated Empress Diadora, and was she now—just another pawn?

Her mind went to the Matrix Experiments and the Truth About Lies documentary—the cost/benefit analysis of lying. Cole had big stakes in the game on this planet. What was the tipping point for him? For him to be the ruler? Of the skies or the seas? Could it have been a ploy? To prove something to Stefanos? Or to Diadora? He had access to all sides—he could have planted the toxins in the Upperworld waters as well as the poison in the Grotto. And, he was the only one who could. She shook off the notion. This man had just saved her from a certain death.

"Parker, I really have to go. We'll talk more. I think you could use some rest, don't you? Maybe clean-up, too?"

"Are you implying I'm a mess?"

"I don't have to imply anything. We'll take up where we left off later." He winked and disappeared into a layer of cloud cover.

She still warmed from the touch of Cole's body next to hers and tried to erase the warning signal in her brain. Parker cleared her head and backtracked her way to Edison and Henley.

"What was that all about, Parker?" Henley asked.

"All what about?"

Henley gave her a knowing smirk. "You know, you and Cole.".

"I just wanted to say thank you." She knew they had witnessed the embrace and was grateful neither said more. "I can't believe he's going back there."

"Now, listen up, Parker," Edison said. "No tears. I don't want any of us getting sentimental. We made a pact. We have a way to go, but we have a job to do. Promise me we're going to save these people, and then make it home."

"Before they tear each other apart," Henley added.

chapter twenty-six

After a few days of much needed rest and anxious to test the purification theories, Parker wanted to put their project into place on Katamoor. She would not linger on the terror below the Spyridon Sea, but she would keep a close watch on Cole.

She holed up for the week in the lab with Edison and Henley reviewing the requirements for each phase of the project. The night had turned jet black and Edison had taken a break. He focused out the window and said, "Do you think these are the same stars in the sky at home? I want to feel like we are connected to Earth."

"Yeah. We are, if you recall, there's this thing called a portal," Henley teased. "I'd say it's a direct connect if there ever was one."

"I mean, more like a connection in our galaxy. Our universe. On a night like tonight, the stars would be out and we'd be grilling in the backyard. My relatives would be over. We're a big bunch. Makes me sad." He lowered his gaze. "I just hope my family doesn't think a car hit me and

I'm dead now. It was the last thing I remember before I arrived here. Do you think it's true?"

"What's true?" Parker asked.

"What Stefanos said—time would pass, but it would only be moments had elapsed when we returned. I hope so."

"He hasn't let us down yet. I believe him." Parker went quiet, pensive, and said, "Let's stop thinking about home, it will be daylight before we know it. Comes so fast here. And you both got so much done while I have been a jailbird! Now it just needs to work."

Henley snorted. "Jailbird! I thought I had a monopoly on bird-based comedy."

"Take a look at this Parker," Edison said. He handed over a list full of cross-outs and scratch-offs. "I hope my second-guessing is accurate. I think we have answers, but so much guess-work."

She brushed her long brown hair aside and wiped the moisture from her brow and the beading behind her neck, thinking there's no getting used to the heat here. Was this how Earth would be one day—like the tropics, or worse, the heat of the equator with no way to cool off? If she ever did get home, she would be listening to the media reports on climate change very differently. More than that, she would put all her knowledge and effort into doing something about it.

She added, "Edison, I can't believe you lined up all the regions to come here to meet with us. You can do anything!"

"Not only can he do anything—he can also get anyone to do anything he wants, Parker," Henley said. "They even get along with me. Miracle of miracles."

"You're not that bad, Henley," Parker said. "It's all about survival for everyone in the Upperworld—not to mention us too."

"Time will tell. And not on my time." Henley broke into the conversation. "I'm home as soon as this membrane gets put together. I'm okay being a hero and saving the world and all, but I need some crab rangoon, stat."

"Henley," Parker interjected, "Speaking of the membrane, I've spent the last few hours reviewing the schematics of the purification system and the woven layers make sense. Maybe you're right, Edison—I know it sounds bizarre, but maybe they needed us to come here to make this happen. Either of you have any last-minute doubts?"

"Nope. But if you really are asking about doubts, I doubt everything!" Henley replied.

"Yeah. This planet, with all its peculiarities, isn't as it appears," Edison said. "You'd think with just clouds and branches, for the most part, we'd have nothing to work with. But with the help of the regions and the bounty from the Virago Trees, we have many options—chemical purifiers, adhesives, and flexible fibers, everything we need. Stuff indigenous to Katamoor, just waiting for someone to put it together for them. They may be smart with heightened perception, but they just might have missed it."

"Hard to see the forest from the trees when you are living it every day I guess." Henley held her hands up in mock defense. "None of this would have happened without all three of us knocking our heads together."

chapter twenty-seven

"What was it like, Edison, figuring stuff out, working with the Upperworlders? Did you understand everything they said?" Parker asked as she scanned his list of groups and the materials they had been assigned.

"Strange at first, but then I realized even though they look different than us, they are just another species. Like we are to them. And smart too! I got used to it after a while."

She peered out the glass wall. "Did they just show up, or how did they make appointments with you—how did you know how to communicate with them?"

"They sorta just come when they come. And usually at first light. They mark time so differently. They send a cardinal a day ahead as a sign they will be arriving, just at the break of dawn. You know cardinals are mystical in the avian world. Even at home, they are considered messengers from beyond. And like clockwork, the dedicated project leaders arrive the following day. And sure enough, I'd wake up and find them waiting here for me. Right at daybreak."

Parker pointed to a line on the sheet with her finger, "Your schedule says the Condors are coming today. It's just about daybreak."

"Yeah, they are coming from the North Sky. It's a haul. But trust me, they'll be right on time."

"Parker," Henley said, "I'm gonna prepare you because the first time I saw them up close, without the bright lights shining in my eyes, whoa, I was floored."

"What do you mean?"

"They are more human than they appear on the surface. They talk, reason, emote. It takes a bit to get used to the humanity coming from the body a bird. But it's pretty cool."

"And guess what, like clockwork—here they are." Edison announced.

Large shadows filled the glass window and the room dimmed.

Parker drew in her breath, awed by the massive size of the species. She picked out the leader by instinct. The largest of the group, almost the size of Stefanos, stepped forward. Groomed black feathers with a lacey frill of white feathers circled the bird's neckline, tuxedo-style. Funny, Parker thought—their feathers match up with their formal mannerisms. Reserved, but polite and cooperative.

Parker knew they must be worried. The Condor region had suffered severe losses due to the poisoned waters. Any water thought to be clean needed to travel hundreds of miles north to their territories, and any mistake meant deaths. Their nesting locations had been destroyed by unrest. Food sources limited by lack of sufficient water resulted in hundreds of Condors sick and dying in the airy nests of the north. Their survival at stake, this project had to work for them, too.

Parker must've been down in prison longer than she thought, because these Condors were massive. Their huge feathered bodies, up to ten feet tall, concealed their truly unthinkable wingspans. The feathers went white around their neck, and ended there, making them appear somewhat like wrinkled priests.

The giant Condor directed its comments to Edison, "We are here to present our findings for the bonding material." The Condor leader sported a fleshy caruncle with folds upon folds that rattled with each word.

"We have traversed the North Sky and found what you requested. There are a handful of places where fibrous grasses grow, where the land is barely covered by water, and my people have tested out the varietals. We have sourced a few good alternatives. Each works, but we have our favorite." Four smaller Condors lifted a large bag and placed it in front of Edison.

"This is our first choice—a flexible fiber with an adhesive quality. It will bond well with the Virago root system you described. We performed initial testing. I am convinced you will not find better. These fibrous leaves grow naturally among our rubber tree twigs and branches in the peaks of the North Sky. We are confident we can obtain as much as you require."

With clipped, stubby talons, the Condor presented several samples of the flexible cording and placed it in front of them.

"We have an alternate as well." The Condor presented a twisted rope cording, also with a glue-like quality. "I like this option too but fear the stability of the roping will break down over time in saltwater. Our recommendation is the flexible fiber."

As the meeting progressed, Parker relaxed. Edison and Henley had done more than she had expected. Their process had been methodical. As each regional group passed through, one by one, Parker became even more confident their plan was strong.

Henley hailed Parker over to meet the Skuas with a bunch of cute tail feathers poking from under their short little robes. As Henley made introductions, Parker took in the lean and limber bodies and agile form.

"Parker, these are the Skuas. They will work with the Weavers to construct the system. The Skuas are well-suited for the underwater construction. They move like acrobats," Henley explained. "Have you ever seen how a gull dips into the top of the water to feed? Well, we're going to have the Skuas dive bomb; it's their specialty. They'll set up near the surface of the sea, and dive beneath the waters to help the weavers thread the membrane."

"I'm impressed," she said.

Henley snorted. "Didn't I tell you I was a genius? Think you've got the market cornered on brains?"

"Humble, too," Edison added.

The last two groups arrived together. Parker returned Henley's broad smile. Though Henley appeared tough on the outside, she cared deeply about this project. Parker thought Henley's dad would be proud of her—she would make a great engineer.

"Parker, meet the Raptors and the Titans. They'll both play an important role. I introduced them as the 'clinchers' in the engineering plan." Henley said. "They'll ensure what we build will stand the test of time."

"We are known for our keen vision, the best in the Upperworld," the leader of the Raptors spoke from a long, curved beak. "We can see perfectly under virtually any condition, including total darkness or smoke." The bird extended a strong talon directly to the center of Parker's eye before changing direction and then shooting a bright red beam toward the far end of the lab. Parker flinched, at first taken aback by another species with pyrokinetic ability. These powerful skills had certainly helped them stay alive she thought as she watched a hole burn into the filmy wall. "You can tell this is not so dainty an ability."

She wondered why they didn't use the skills to protect themselves from the Underworld. Instinctively she knew the answer—they were not an aggressive culture. They wanted peace.

"Our vision guides our talons." The Raptor leader continued, "The beam will bond each juncture point of the membrane. They'll be no weak link in our system."

Our system? Parker glanced at Henley and Edison. The plan belonged to everyone in the Upperworld, not just the three of them, just as Stefanos had wanted.

Parker's bracelet began pulsing as the leader of the Titans moved toward her. He represented the last of the regions to present, and he didn't wait for Henley to make introductions.

The huge, hulking form towered over her, cloaked in an orange-brown robe with pale and mottled lapels.

"I am Cranwell, leader of the Titans," he stated. "Parker, the last time I saw you, I had my doubts. I thought to myself, she's such a young girl. These humans are children facing an impossible task. How will they accomplish this? But I reminded myself, our Sky King has an uncanny way of surprising us all. Even you, I'm sure."

The air around her took on the honey sweet fragrance. Parker peeked behind her. Belliza had arrived, filling Parker with hope all would be okay.

"I'm here to assure you all," Cranwell said, "the Titans will protect the waters and the area surrounding the Virago Trees during construction. We'll safeguard the materials and protect our people until the project is complete. The Titans are the guardians of the Upperworld, and I have committed my warriors to this task. We will be on the prowl for any danger lurking in our path."

Belliza neared Parker's side, and the familiar sense of well-being enveloped Parker. The hummingbird gathered the group around her. "I will be delivering your planz to Ztefanoz now. He will review and give you hiz decizion tonight."

Belliza unraveled the bundle she carried in her beak.

"Theze are for you. All of you. They are your ceremonial gownz. Ztefanoz wantz you to wear them when you meet with the Great Onez."

Parker unfolded the white material of the sheath, practically identical to the one with the golden feather trim she had worn when she first arrived. Why did Stefanos want her to wear it now? With mixed emotions she wondered—if Stefanos was sending them home.

"The meeting with the Great Onez will be underway zhortly. The future of Zpyridon will be revealed tonight. Ztefanoz will prezent hiz decizion and we will know if your plan iz approved."

Belliza hovered in the air, her movements steady and slowing. Her honeysuckle mist took over the lab. Her ceaseless buzzing calmed. Parker wondered if Belliza could be connecting to the Spirits of the Sky. Who were these spirits with powers potent enough to comfort Stefanos and right the wrongs taking place in the Upperworld? Parker heard a faint repetitive ululation, "Whooo. Whooo. Whooo."

chapter twenty-eight

Parker counted the days in Spyridon time. It had been three months since they arrived. The pace had slowed, and a sense of safety slowly crept back in. While Stefanos and his investigation turned up nothing, no other violence had come hurtling out of the skies or sucking any of them down into the deeps. She moved with confidence, flanked by Edison and Henley, toward the Great Hall.

"I'm nervous. Are you?" Henley admitted with unusual shyness.

"It'd be pretty crazy if we weren't," Edison said. "This is us becoming heroes...or, you know, scrapping everything and starting over. I'm nervous and so wired. It's like I stuck my finger in an electric socket, that is if they had them here. I don't even want to think of any possibility except Stefanos being good with this. Or better yet, if he would only say, we've done enough, and we can leave NOW! I don't mean to doubt our abilities, but we need everything to go right. And how often does that happen?"

"Don't go there! No doubts today or any day until we're done," Parker burst out. "I'm serious."

"Okay. I have a confession, though," Henley offered. "I've been debating whether to tell you guys."

Parker and Edison slowed their steps.

"I heard something I probably wasn't meant to," Henley said. "Cole said to Belliza he didn't think Stefanos would like our idea."

Parker had witnessed the exchange between Belliza and Cole and had been surprised Cole appeared visibly worried. He'd spoken softly to Belliza, warning her they needed to tread carefully. Henley had picked up the same conversation. She wondered how Henley could've heard from so far away. Then again, she wondered how Edison could calm someone just with humming, or how she had begun to master flying around without Belliza's guidance.

"Cole said, 'Peace for the Underworld?' and he was worried. He said, 'You know Stefanos won't be in favor of that,'" Henley said.

"Did Belliza answer him?" Edison asked.

"No."

"Well, we'll know soon enough," Parker said. "But I have to believe because our project is happening on the Upperworld's sacred land, we must have the Spirits on our side. I know we're doing science here, but I believe the key to their survival—and ours—is the holiness on Katamoor and the Virago Trees." Parker stopped walking, thinking aloud, "I might be out of my mind, but I wonder if the Spirits sent us this idea."

"I don't care who sent the idea as long as it works," Henley said.

"Let's remember our pact." They fist-bumped and walked into the Great Hall.

Stefanos already in position, held court at the Ruling Perch. He acknowledged their entrance with a tip of his beak. He'd kept his distance since their return. Now, he posed regally above his leaders in the Great Hall, much like on the night of the attack. Belliza hovered at his side. A rung lower, Vibius and Cole formed a base of solidarity and support.

Parker's heart leapt from her chest and she sighed with relief knowing Cole had returned safely from the Underworld. She glanced about the Great Hall, shocked by the number of Great Ones in attendance. She calculated the rows and perches, estimating there must be at least five hundred Great Ones in attendance.

She scanned the room for familiar faces. Poised on the uppermost perches in the highest row, the leaders and representatives from the Condors and the Raptors. Closer in, almost next to Vibius and Cole, were the Titans, the Passeri, and Skuas. Cranwell caught her eye and she was comforted by his proximity. He'd been a tireless and faithful companion during the process.

Stefanos opened his wings, nodded his beak, and signaled the meeting would begin.

"My Great Ones, you all know why we are here today. It is with pride I am able to convey the approval of the design and construction of the Mangrove System—a powerful tool—and the key to our survival."

Parker breathed a sigh of relief and side-eyed Edison and Henley.

Stefanos gestured the earthlings to rise. At once, three beams of light bathed each of their bodies.

"Our earthlings have worked with representatives from far and wide across the Upperworld," Stefanos said. "I commend you on your efforts. What has been proposed is a tribute to all of you and your cooperation. You have developed a plan that will bring us a source for clean water, and it is exactly where it should be—on Katamoor, at the site of our sacred Virago Trees.

Parker listened, but her thoughts kept repeating—she stood in the blinding light again! She repeated over and over in her head—they were safe, the security was tight, and nothing would go wrong. A few more days and they would be back on Earth.

Cole caught her eye and tipped her a wink.

"Through the Mangrove membrane you developed with our human team, not only will the Virago Trees give us a sustainable, never-ending source of clean water, but we will potentially be able to extend the existing landmass for our world and grow even more Viragos."

The filmy walls shook with the vibration of thunderous applause. Stefanos silenced the Great Ones with another wave of his wing.

"We will have clean water," he continued. "And, more importantly, we will survive independently of those in the Underworld who would wish us ill. The work will begin tomorrow. The plans will be circulated and posted across the kingdom tonight. All will know their role and their duties."

The thunderous cry again went up. "Sky King! Sky King! Sky King!"

chapter twenty-nine

Once a peaceful refuge for Upperworlders seeking spirituality, the sacred, swampy land on Katamoor had been transformed into a hub of activity. The materials had been transported to floating barge-like structures at points along the shores of the continent. Within a two-mile radius of the land mass, all who approached—by air or by sea—were stopped and credentials checked before permission to enter was granted.

At all times, the Titans stood watch. Endless days were filled with the buzz of camaraderie until twilight deepened and faded to black. Only then would the caws and the shouting of orders from the workforce cease for the brief respite before rising to work again at dawn.

Parker wrapped her arm around Henley's shoulder. "I can't believe how quickly this is coming together—having the Weavers ready to pounce when the divers laid out the materials—pretty cool! How did you know this would work?"

"I'd like to say I just knew, but I feel like I don't know

anything anymore. I think Edison hums genius into my brain." Henley smiled a self-congratulatory grin. "And of course, those old Spirits of the Sky. We must have them on our side."

Henley laughed but Parker didn't believe her for a second. She didn't care, though; she preferred the happy Henley—the one who laughed at the good spirits, the ones in the sky or otherwise.

"Let's find Edison. I think he's up ahead working on securing the membrane with the Akkas."

Parker looped her arm around Henley's. They strode through the darkness arm in arm as they traversed the swampy ground, the night stars already out and illuminating a shadowy path. Despite the foreboding in her head, Parker relaxed with the new glow of connecting to someone her age and feeling comfortable.

Henley tilted her head, forcing her jet-black hair to fall to one side. She stopped walking.

"What's the matter?" Parker asked.

Henley held her hand up for silence and mouthed, Shhhh. "Listen, it's Edison." From beyond the rustle of the wind, Edison's tune rose through the air as if riding the wind. Parker's worry eased. She breathed in the sweet sounds.

"His voice is unlike any other," Henley said, "I used to think I could sing. I thought I knew everything about music. But he's a song-whisperer. I can't tell if it's the sound or the vibration. Either way, it's a little mystical.

"Did you know I sing, too?" Henley stammered. "I

think you know a lot about us. I keep thinking about the night I ended up here. I just wanted to escape my life. Make a name for myself. I told you about the band. I kept seeing myself on a tour bus, traveling the country, leaving my parents and all their rules behind. I couldn't wait to get away. Now I just want to go back. Feel safe."

"We will, Henley. We're close now. I want to be home, too. Everyone hated me at school. They all thought I was a nerd. They called me names and I felt left out of everything. Kinda like the way you felt about me, Henley."

Henley threw her head back and belted out several loud laughs. "Ya got me there, Parker. Not your fault though. Mine. I didn't want to be here. And you only tried to make me feel everything would work out. I didn't care. I just wanted out. Now…I've kinda grown to like this place."

"I know. Both you and Edison were giving me the evil eye. I always felt weird around my classmates. I didn't have any friends. I just wanted to escape too—go to college and become a scientist, hide in a lab somewhere. My parents never knew how I felt either. Now I wish I had told them."

"Really, Parker? You? No friends? Kinda hard to believe." She laughed. "Everyone likes you. Especially a certain someone…"

She knew Henley was referring to Cole and changed the subject. "I'd like to hear you sing sometime."

Henley blinked at the abrupt change of subject. "Right now, I can't even think about that Parker. It makes me sad."

"Okay. Let's listen to Edison. He'll make us both feel better."

"I wish we could but there's no rest tonight. The Weavers just need to complete the netting of the membrane, secure it, and our fibers and root system become one. And I can't believe I am going to say this, but we'll be done. We can pack our bags for home. Oh wait, I forgot, we don't have any bags. You think they'll throw us a party?"

"The biggest party in recent history, I'd guess."

Parker couldn't see Henley's bright smile in the dark, but she felt it shine.

chapter thirty

Stefanos shot an eagle eye glare at Parker when she entered the Roost. She frowned and tried to unspool the reason for the summons and his distasteful expression. Belliza, positioned in the corner of the room, remained aloof. Hmmm, something's up, and it wasn't good.

The Roost, now devoid of sound, only a hint of the light rustle of the Sky King's robe. Parker, perplexed by the silence and Belliza's atypical distance, waited, determined not to speak first. The quiet tortured her. This was Stefanos' domain, and he had demanded her appearance. Let him begin the conversation.

With abrupt directness, he finally spoke. "I am not in favor of your plan. Contrary to what I voiced to the Great Ones. I wanted to raise my objections without an audience to save your embarrassment."

Parker's heart dropped to her stomach.

"I cannot justify these drastic changes on Katamoor when the Underworld will benefit. They will thrive at our expense. That was not the goal." His voice remained at a monotone, yet Parker knew his tone belied his feelings. "I have kept the Underworld at bay. They are in their place, where they belong. We've sustained controlled peace." As he spoke, his feathers trembled—his agitation more evident. "And now, you decide to help them? You were ordered to help the Upperworld!"

Parker retreated to her shell.

"Now, the Underworld will have light?" His feathers fluttered and rose perpendicular to his body. His eyes squinted. "I am not stupid, and I am beginning to think you may presume I am. This filter you have developed for the Viragos will reduce the murkiness of the waters of the Underworld. It will permit essential light to reach their ecosystems and aid in survival of the Underworld and the whole of the species below the sea. Perhaps, even better for them than for us."

"But, wouldn't that be good for the planet?" Parker asked.

"Why would I want the Underworld to flourish! How will I ever be able to protect our world? Was our war for nothing? We survived the devastation of our planet. We evolved and constructed a way to live simpler lives. And now the evil lurking below us, those who seek to harm us, will be able to cross into our world? Not acceptable!"

Tears gathered in her eyes as she struggled to fight them back.

He continued to ramble, like a runaway train propelled by its own motion. "You must put an end to this, Parker.

You can help us clean and protect our water sources, but only for us. You will find an alternative, and quickly. My time is waning. I will not be here to protect my people or you for much longer. I will not permit this plan to continue." He cast a shadowy frost at Belliza, daring her to move. "And you! You Belliza, you brought this on by giving Parker your mother's bracelet."

The little bird quivered. Parker stood in shock as she witnessed Stefanos disfavor Belliza.

Parker tried to understand what brought about this frightful change in Stefanos. Was this the first time Belliza noticed he had lost control? His behavior appeared uncharacteristic—at least from the short amount of time she had come to know him.

Belliza didn't reply. Stefanos grimaced. "Parker would never have been able to untangle the web of the Virago Trees. With the amulet, Parker has found her power. She will learn how to control it. And before her time! You knew this could happen, Belliza! You think you can just give this power to the young earthling without my knowledge? You gave it to her while in the Underworld. You know my vision is blocked below the Spyridon Sea. Is that why you chose to give it to her there? So, she could usurp my power?"

Belliza turned away, casting her beak down.

"Do not lie to me, Belliza!" His voice shook the air.

Belliza found the courage to speak. "I never planned on giving Parker the amulet. When we were in the Underworld and I thought I heard zcreaming in the

Grotto, I felt rezponzible. Nothing muzt happen to her. Zhe needed the protection and I thought zhe could benefit more than me from the powerz. Zhe will need it for the future. The amulet can only help thoze with the power. You and I both know Parker'z power comez from within her. The amulet can only zhow her what iz already inzide.

"Ztefanoz, at firzt, thiz waz about our zurvival. But the earthlingz have zhown me we can make thingz better. Pleaze hear me out. We muzt think about zaving our planet firzt—the whole planet, not juzt the Upperworld. It'z the only way we will all zurvive."

As Belliza spoke, Parker saw Stefanos' eyes narrow, scrutinizing the hummingbird's every word.

"Parker'z plan opened my eyez to other wayz we can live, zide by zide. You can lead the way, Zky King, for all of Zpyridon, reztore our planet. Frezh water for uz. More land for uz. Light for the Underworld, which will help plant life thrive. We all will be better off–"

Stefanos' eyes widened, stopping Belliza mid-sentence. He breathed, almost inaudibly, "No..."

Without another word, Stefanos soared to the height of the Roost. A fierce rumble erupted. Had Stefanos shaken the whole of the Citadel? Or were the tremors in the Roost a physical reverberation of his anger?

The filmy walls of the Roost shook and swayed. He beat his wings, and Parker felt the unseen hand of his power take hold of her.

The thrust shot Parker up to the height of the Roost. Stefanos dropped beneath her to catch her in his wings, steadying himself as the castle walls quaked. From within his grasp, Parker lifted her head to find the horizon outside the glass walls, searching desperately for the isle of Katamoor and the Virago Trees. A veil of smoke curled and smothered the tiny island. Blazing eruptions of fire shot high into the air above the smoky cloud cover.

Explosions! Was the Underworld attacking them again?

The sea surrounding the continent bubbled and foamed. The waves of the Spyridon Sea rose higher. They washed up against the reeds and marshes and onto the shores. The Virago Trees shook violently. Shockwaves from the explosives ripped limbs off. The anger of the rising waves submerged the island, the perimeter dipping below sea level. Parker feared the landmass would disappear entirely.

Fragments of bone and feathers flew everywhere. Bodies plummeted into the sea. Debris, tree limbs, particles of fiber and membrane littered the air, the sea, and what remained of Katamoor. Stefanos peered out of the largest glass wall and closed his eyes. Parker sensed he was communicating with his leaders.

Moments later Vibius appeared.

"You summoned me, Great Sky King?" a battle-weary Vibius said between breaths, as he swooped into the Roost. His wings quivered visibly as he landed. Parker worried about the poor soul. He moved as if in shock and carried the smells of the Katamoor wetlands. His robe splattered with a dusty grey gunpowder.

"Where have you been, Vibius? I hope you were not caught in the explosions in Katamoor." Stefanos asked, scanning his debris covered feathers.

"Yes, I nearly got hit, within a fraction of an inch. The Spirits must have watched out for me, Sky King. I had been overjoyed by the progress. Then, this tragic turn, our poor sacred Virago Trees." He wept and dried his eyes with his talon and cried out loud, "Fate tossed us an unexpected blow. A travesty. All the bodies tumbling into the sea. I don't understand." The poor elderly hawk's incoherent, Parker thought. "Diadora would never do this! Why? Why?" His eyes blurred, and he wore a dazed expression. "You know all, Great Sky King. Why would the Spirits of the Sky abandon us?"

"War changes us. We know that. There must be a reason for this," Stefanos had somehow returned to his former self, fortified with strength and regal power. "The Spirits know more than we do. We must keep our faith. We must carry on."

He eyed Belliza and with a wave of his talon dismissed Vibius. "You are a good soldier, Great Vibius. You need your rest. I'll call for you when the Titans and the rest of our leaders arrive. They should be here shortly. I'll need you by my side then."

Stefanos turned back to Parker. "I was not in favor of your project Parker, but this is worse than any of my fears. I wanted a peaceful resolution. I hoped you would understand my concern about the Underworld." He shook his great head and muttered, "...the holiest place on our planet! We must right what has gone wrong, at whatever the cost."

Parker, caught in the embrace of his wings, whispered, "Sky King I know your heart is good. You only wanted what was best. But, please, I must go and see if Edison and Henley are all right."

His feathers were moist with sweat. He relaxed his grip on her. "I await your return, Parker. May the Spirits be with you. Be safe."

chapter thirty-one

Parker trekked through the soaking wet weeds and grasses, choking on the smoke-filled air as she searched for Henley and Edison. The scaffolding rigged by the Weavers had collapsed in the mud. Blood-splattered dead bodies, piled on top of one another, lay scattered next to the broken tree limbs. Parker couldn't bear to think of all those she had come to know and work with—those who now lay dead before her. And how many others had fallen into the sea?

Her eyes, vacant, unfocused and blurry, took in the destruction of life—a large Condor bleeding profusely from a huge gash on its wing, a group of small Skuas, mourning over their dead. She couldn't look, but she couldn't tear her eyes away either. Seeing all those who had perished hurt to depths she hadn't realized she possessed. Through the smoke, she spotted Henley and Edison working side by side. They were clearing a space for triage among the burned-out Virago Trees, hoisting the wounded to small platforms they layered on the higher limbs.

In the midst of the horror, Parker's heart swelled realizing her two companions' concerns focused on helping others. Her head buzzed and her eyes continued to water. She picked her way through the mire of tangled, falling trees and corpses. She called out their names, her voice cracking. Shaking and out of control, her body fought off the panic. She inched toward Henley, snapping the burnt tree limbs in her path.

Through quivering lips, she said, "I have no words..." Parker clung to Henley to make sure she was real.

"Me neither," Henley said. She wore a blank, dazed expression.

They stood inches from Edison, but he didn't notice. Parker pulled him into her chest and leaned close to his ear. "Squeeze my hands, can you hear me?" Parker asked. And thankfully, he had the presence of mind to do so. They held each other without speaking while the sinking, muddy ground quaked beneath them.

Edison finally released words in a jumble of grief. "My heart is tearing in half. I hurt everywhere." He began to cry. "We made so much progress..."

"We're alive." Parker said. "We have each other. We'll get through this." Parker wanted to believe her words, but her faith dwindled. "We promised each other we wouldn't give up."

Edison solemnly nodded and collected himself. "What could have happened this time? After being in the Underworld, I wouldn't doubt this attack came from them. But they would have known this would help them. And give them more light." He added slowly, "I hate to say this but, could they have planned this when they discovered you escaped?"

"I was thinking the same thing. I just didn't want to say it. To make it true. Then, it would all be my fault," Parker said.

"Not your fault people go nuts when they can't wrongfully execute someone." Edison gave a rueful chuckle. "That's not on you."

Henley pulled away, shivering. "I'm glad you are here with us. I'm glad we got you out of the Underworld. No matter the cost."

Henley's words gave Parker the strength to smile. "I'd say breathe deeply but who can breathe this air? At least we didn't get hurt. We haven't been hit. Now maybe we can help these poor creatures."

Together they went about seeking those who were unhurt by the attacks and put them to work to help the others who weren't as fortunate. She, Edison and Henley reconnected with the Titans, and began to coordinate relief.

Throughout the grim work, Parker couldn't help ruminating about the failure of their project. More and more, it appeared the one who had attacked the Great Hall at the beginning of all this must be the same one responsible for this latest attack. Could this shadowy figure also be behind the deaths of Pantione and the royal family? Parker suspected the answer was yes.

That meant someone playing both sides against one

another. The person in the best position to do so appeared to be Cole, a possibility that hurt her too much to think about. Cole had saved her life, endured torture for her. Surely, he couldn't be capable of such violence.

Cole also could have kept the identity of the perpetrator from becoming known. If he had been in the best position to do the deeds, he'd also have been in the best position to discover the criminal. If the culprit were an Underworlder, wouldn't Cole have found them?

Her head swirled with possibilities. Stefanos should have been able to discover any Upperworlder responsible for attacking their own people. But…Stefanos had been preoccupied with Parker and his own belief he wasn't long for this world.

Hours passed. They were miserable, yet uplifting hours of finding survivors, helping nurse them to health, and uncovering sections of their filtration project undamaged. She hoped beyond hope, with time and opportunity, they'd piece their efforts back together and find the saboteur before they destroyed any hope of peace permanently.

A sudden jolt of electricity ran through her. Parker sensed something behind her and spun around. Appearing like an apparition, Cole moved through the debris like a ghost on a mission. He was covered in soot and his skin marked with blood and scorch marks. He wandered through the haze lost until his eyes met Parker's and linked. In one swift motion, he bolted toward her, lifted her in the air, and carried her in his arms to the hidden shadows of the scattered limbs of a toppled mangrove. He drew her toward his firm body and the space between them closed. His mouth sought hers.

She had never been kissed before. Her lips were stiff at first. His mouth pressed deeper and her heart danced. His supple lips softened hers and lingered. Then he abruptly pulled away.

"I don't know what came over me, Parker. I should never have done that." Unable to meet her eyes, he stammered, "I'm sorry. I couldn't stop myself."

"Cole, look into my eyes."

He did, and she saw uncertainty there. Could it be guilt? She prayed not.

"Please tell me if you know who did this."

"I wish I did."

She knew the answer before he had spoken. When he denied the knowledge, she realized something else: she was developing feelings for him, beyond just his words. She had begun to sense the truth of his words. She'd begun to read his thoughts.

She laughed in joyous relief and kissed him again. Caught in the passion of the moment and feeling safe in his arms, Parker curled the corner of her mouth, sending him a mischievous invitation. She cupped his face with her fingers, wiping her mind free of the disaster surrounding them. "Will you kiss me again? Once more."

He leaned in. His mouth covered hers again and a wave of heat spread throughout her body. Butterflies twirled in her stomach. The world stood frozen in time.

Wrapped in his arms, she felt protected. Maybe even loved. The catastrophe surrounding them faded and all she saw, all she felt, was Cole. She pressed her lips firmly into his until they blended into one. Her hands rested on his cheeks, and ran over his upper back, and touched his wings, caressing the light feathers softly.

The imprint of his lips remained on hers. He whispered, "Parker, I know I said this before, but I feel a deep connection to you."

"When I first met you, I felt you were more like us than them." Her words stammered out, muffled in his chest. Their conversation felt so new. She never had spoken like this with anyone, especially a boy. But she wanted the talk to continue. "When we were in the Grotto, watching Pantione with his family, I was scared. I felt we didn't belong there. But then I looked at you and felt okay. I felt the same way when I first saw you—when you came to the Citadel. My worries vanish when I am with you. Just like now."

He was quiet for a while and she began to think she had said too much.

"Funny you should say that," he said, wiping his brow and clearing the grit from his face.

"Say what?"

"I never felt quite like anyone on Spyridon either," he said, after a slight pause. "Before you arrived, I thought this is just the way the world is. I can't even remember meeting anyone in my entire lifetime like me. I've been here so long. At first, I wondered, if the attraction I felt was because I am more human, like you, than those in the Upperworld or Underworld."

Her eyes dropped down, suddenly embarrassed by the intimacy of sharing feelings.

"What's going to happen now, Cole?" she asked. "Everything we've built is lost. All of our planning has been for nothing."

"I have a plan. And it will work. Everything has changed for me, Parker." He relaxed his hold on her but did not pull away. He lifted her chin with his index finger and his bright blue eyes took in her face. "I've made up my mind. I'm not going to be a go-between for the Sky King and the Empress any longer. When I am around the Empress, I wait for her to unlock my secret. No longer. She will learn the truth about me. Now. It is the only way to make things right."

She wanted to interrupt, to ask him what he meant. But she waited to see where his thoughts led him.

"I have struggled to support our Sky King's agenda, and only his agenda, as I believe he has been mostly fair. But war is war, and in this case, it is not just for the Upperworld, or for the Underworld, but for Spyridon. When the Upperworld won the last war, Stefanos held the Underworld at bay. Our people were safe from the brutality of the Underworld leaders like Kendrick, who only wanted to destroy us. But Diadora's position is different. I know she understands there is a whole planet at stake."

He was silent and she moved closer in as he said, "I'm

not going to tell you it has nothing to do with you, because some of what I am feeling does. You helped validate what I have known all along."

After an effortful pause, he changed the subject. "Let's go back to Edison and Henley. I just needed this moment with you. I need to know they are ok, too. Let's find them."

Cole followed Parker to the triage area where Edison and Henley still worked alongside a group of storks who were airlifting injured bodies to higher ground.

"How are you holding up?" Cole asked.

Edison shrugged his shoulders and sighed. "Doin' okay. Better than our crew. They took the brunt. They didn't deserve this."

Henley asked, "What will happen, Cole?"

"Stefanos will want to retaliate. Though we can't be certain it was the Underworld. I discussed the filtration system with the Empress, and I believe she is amenable," Cole said. "Makes me think someone, other than the Underworld ruler, maybe one of her captains, has a plan of their own. She is young, but she is tough. But her actions are never lethal without provocation. She would be more thoughtful than this. And as she told us at the onset, she would have announced her intentions at first strike."

Silence took over Katamoor. Even the bird cries and cackles had ceased. The old shell of silence quelled Parker's voice. No one spoke.

"So, there is going to be a war?" Edison asked.

"I think it has already begun." Cole wore a grave expression. "I am going back to join Stefanos at the Roost.

The Underworld is planning their strategy now. If we can't put an end to this, there will be nothing left of Spyridon, and Stefanos is well aware of that. All of you, wait for me in the Sky Box. I will come back to you when we have finished."

"One thing, Cole," Parker said as Cole turned to leave. "I hope I am not out of line in saying this, but the Sky King's behavior is erratic, almost as if he has lost control of his emotions."

Cole listened without speaking. "I will meet you all back in the Sky Box."

Edison said, "Really, Stefanos, out of control? I didn't think things could get any worse."

"Now what do we do?" Henley cried out.

"We've done what we can here. We have to see if we can find out what they are planning."

They returned to the Citadel and went directly to the Roost. A raised, unintelligible dialogue drifted out of Stefanos' inner sanctum. Parker, Edison and Henley peered out the large glass windows to the world of clouds beyond the Roost and the Citadel. The smoke surged from Katamoor, spreading tentacles across the Upperworld, moving toward them. Parker watched in horror as their hard work smoldered.

chapter thirty-two

Cranwell's voice transcended the walls of the Roost where Parker, Edison, and Henley lingered. They strained to hear every word. None of the heated conversation was very clear. But bickering and discord sounded the same in every language.

Then Stefanos' voice boomed with clarity, "None of us want to blame this on Diadora. We have always worked out our disagreements with her. Though impetuous at times, as expected from the youth, we've been able to reason with both her and Pantione. I no longer believe the empty words they delivered at Zonoros Point. We cannot stand by and allow ourselves to be attacked. We must mobilize at once. All troops must be prepared for battle. I've had the Ravens work with the poison we discovered in our water supply, and they've developed a very effective weapon. We will go on the offensive immediately—release our own chemical weaponry, and they will not be able to escape. They will be obliterated. We could have done this long ago, and protected our world, but that is not our culture, not our way. They have crossed the line now. I am at fault for giving them the opportunity to strike. Now, the Underworld will have to pay the price for their actions."

"I second that," Vibius said. "We must not delay. If we react immediately, we will catch them off-guard. We should have escalated this at first strike and not have given them a second opportunity."

The Sky King bellowed, "I am ordering a declaration of war. Tonight!"

Cranwell, the great Titan, stepped forward. "You can say whatever you like, Sky King, but I am not permitting my troops to take part in a full-scale war. And a chemical war! No! I refuse to participate. We've suffered enough loss. We're not even sure who is behind this. No one has claimed responsibility. And we know the Empress would! In fact, she has denied it. A counter-attack is premature."

Cranwell turned his back on Stefanos and stormed out of the inner sanctum. The Titan and the Condor leaders followed, leaving those remaining inside murmuring to one another in uncertainty.

Cole rushed after the leaders, passing Parker without a glance. "We have to solve this, Cranwell. Walking away won't help anything," Cole yelled out to them as they left the Roost, "You know we will come to an agreement. I will make sure of it. There's much here we do not know, but I intend to find out. I stand behind you. And I will find out who is responsible!"

Cranwell stopped at Cole's side and whispered something with urgency before striding out of the Citadel.

He hurried past Parker, Edison, and Henley waiting in the corridor.

Henley frowned and turned to Parker and Edison. "I just heard Cranwell tell Cole that he thinks the Sky King is not himself. He doesn't understand the change in Stefanos' behavior." Henley shook as she repeated Cranwell's words, "he said, 'he's not following Stefanos on a death march.' And then he left to go to his troops. He said he had to stop the bleeding."

Parker hadn't picked up a word between Cole and Cranwell. So, Parker and Edison weren't the only two developing extraordinary abilities the longer they remained here.

Cole strode out of the Roost and past them. He took a double take at Parker, Edison and Henley. He hardened, sending them a frosty stare. He addressed them harshly, "What are you doing here? I told you to wait for me in the Sky Box. Go there. Now."

He took in their expressions and lightened his tone. "And when you get there, seal the door behind you. You have the power to do so, Parker. You'll know what to do."

Cole neared Parker and whispered in her ear, "I'm going to meet up with Cranwell and the Titans and the Condors. And, then I am taking this into my own hands. I have stood by for too long. I am going to confront the Empress. She will learn the truth and I will force them both to compromise. No matter what it takes. If blood must be shed, I will do it myself."

He stopped for a moment and stepped even closer to

Parker, his warm breath on her neck. He touched her face and said, "The madness ends right now."

His fingers brushed against her cheek. As he pulled his hand away, she wished for one more kiss.

chapter thirty-three

Parker stood before the entry to the Sky Box. Her eyes sprinting back and forth between her companions as the burden of the task weighed her down. She had observed Stefanos open and seal the room dozens of times. But now, could she simulate his actions?

Parker pursed her lips, hiding any lingering doubts. Instinctively, she raised her arm, closed her eyes, and independent of voluntary action, a surge of energy claimed her body. Electric currents ran through her veins, thrumming along her bloodstream—the feeling as tactile as if her blood boiled within her. She experimented with a slight upward shift of her index finger and the wall slid open effortlessly. She was controlling the force within her. When she concentrated, her brain triggered the response she wanted. She trembled at the excitement and the power.

Henley gasped. "Holy crap! How did you do that?"

A little scared and a little nervous, Parker stared at her hands as if they were an appendage no longer belonging to her. Parker motioned to Henley and Edison to follow her.

"Come on, let's go in," she said, her hands shaking. Another upward tilt of her finger and the wall closed behind them. Her mind called the electricity to her right hand. Out shot a blaze of fire and the wall of the Sky Box sealed behind them. How was she able to do this? She recognized one thing—whatever was going on within her—through this strength she would be able to keep them safe.

"You've got some magic touch," Edison said. "Parker, it's scary—but I'm not gonna question anything about you anymore. Bring it on!"

"The fire shot out of your fingertips!" Henley backed away from Parker and said, "We saw the Sky King shoot fire with his talon! How are you doing this with your hand?"

"I have no idea. I've never been able to do anything like this before."

Henley shot her a wild glare that said, 'Don't come near me!'

"Don't you think I'm wondering why is this happening now?" Parker stopped and searched their eyes as she rubbed her fingertips. "If you think it's strange to watch me do this, imagine how I feel, when fire comes from my hands and it doesn't burn me? But we'll use these powers to our advantage."

Parker suddenly felt a tug. A flow of energy within her guided her toward the largest glass wall. Weightless, as if a feather blown by the wind, she floated with the current across the room. She swallowed hard. Her mouth dry, layered with a bad taste. Where could this energy flow be coming from? The energy drew her in front of a row of panels which morphed into video screens stretching from one end of the room to the other. She couldn't move, her feet glued in position. Sick to her stomach, the bile and nausea rose within her. She stared at the glass in front of her and watched as a scroll of images appeared on the screen moving at hyper speed. At first, none were distinguishable. Blurred pictures, rapidly crossing the windows, flashed on and off. Voices too. In Chinese.

A woman's voice called out from the screen. "Ming Mei!" Henley moaned in response. Music and chanting played in the background. The images slowed. Center on screen, a poised older Chinese woman, bathed in glorious sunlight, moved about a lovely garden. The woman was arguing with "the moody Henley" Parker first met in the Sky Box. The woman had to be Henley's mother and they must have been at their home in California. She remembered the chant as the one Henley sang when she was worried.

"We've been abducted by a monster!" Henley cried her out to her mom on the screen. She said to Edison and Parker, "I know he brought me—us—here to help them. But the idea he's been watching us all along, waiting to steal our lives away? He stole my life from me! And my poor mother. Oh my God! What must she be thinking—I ran away? I wish I were at home. I should have appreciated my parents only wanted what was best for me! And they were right!"

Tears ran down Henley's cheeks. Parker yearned to

comfort her, yet she could barely comfort herself. She held Henley close and stroked her hair, hoping it would soothe her and said, "We knew they selected us, calm down. They had to have been watching. Stefanos promised us we would not be missing at home. Time travels differently here. Try not to worry." She embraced the sobbing girl wanting to believe her words but finding little comfort.

The force of the screen drew her closer. Parker rotated her hand slightly and the wall now displayed images of Edison walking down a dark city street with a boy who could have been his older brother. The older boy laughed and joked as they walked and talked about basketball. The older boy teased him, "You could be a great forward, bro. Your jump shot's way better than mine! Coach asked me to bring you to practice next week. It'll help you get into college—maybe even help pay for med school."

Edison didn't answer his brother. Parker figured he didn't want to tell him about the choir. Under his breath, Edison softly whispered to Parker, "That's my brother." He said. "Ozzie." Edison winced, lowered his glance. He took a few deep breaths. Anger crossed his face and he shouted to Parker, "I can't watch this. Parker, turn it off! This doesn't help. Can't you just shut it down? Please!"

"I hope so. I'm trying." Parker said, realizing they'd all fall apart if they thought about their lives and the lost opportunities. She tilted her wrist, hoping to close the gap in the floor and end the nightmare of what they had left behind.

But instead, the image display revolved to picture New

York City. Sky-high buildings and Central Park. A lump formed in her throat as she thought about her own home and her parents. She tried to swallow, but the lump wouldn't move.

The images streamed Parker in school—lunch in the cafeteria with the 'Tates' eating together, joking, laughing, bantering with the popular boys sitting next to them. Parker seated at a table alone, had her head buried in a book.

The screen flipped and displayed city streets, horns blaring, traffic jammed for miles, wrapping the FDR on the East Side and jamming the West Side Highway along the Hudson River. Roadways, like parking lots, overflowed onto the bridges and into the tunnels at a dead halt. Planes circled the skies. Factories puffed out steaming smoke. The view zoomed out, and displayed Earth covered in layers of smog.

"But what does all of this mean? And what does that have to do with us?" Edison asked.

Parker's focus shifted to Belliza. She needed to bring the hummingbird to the Sky Box. She wanted to talk to her. A few moments later, Belliza appeared drained and exhausted outside the glass wall. Parker unsealed the Sky Box and the little bird flew in and slumped before them. Parker read sadness in Belliza's eyes.

"Belliza, you need to tell us what happened. What's going on right now?" Edison demanded. "You brought us here, then you abandoned us."

The hummingbird didn't answer, and Parker

understood why. She read the bird's thoughts—Belliza was unable to speak. Why hadn't she seen this earlier? Belliza didn't want Parker to know her loyalties were divided. Belliza had chosen to stay true to Stefanos and he'd…what? Put some sort of silence spell on her? Commanded her to silence? No…

"Don't be angry with Belliza, Edison. None of this is her fault. She cannot speak against the Sky King. I can read her eyes," Parker said. Parker thought back to when she first arrived everything was a puzzle. Now, she had begun to understand the Upperworlders and what was on their minds.

Edison sighed. "There has to be a place on this planet where we can get away from Stefanos and plan our next move. I don't know what he'll do when he finds us here. I know you said we are safe now, Parker. But what if Stefanos is still powerful enough to break through? What if he kills us?"

Parker locked arms with Edison and Henley. Belliza hovered over Parker's shoulder.

"He wouldn't," Parker replied. "We are his hope for the future. He won't do anything to harm us. There are more important ways we can contribute. I have a different idea of what he wants from us."

"Spill it! We're on borrowed time until that wall opens up and someone starts shooting fire at us!" Edison said. "I'm telling you both now—if anyone breaks in here, they'll be some dead birds. I am not afraid."

As Edison spoke, the flow of images began to roll

again, this time independent of Parker. Peculiar markings appeared in a shifting pattern of angular scratches on a dark background.

What was this artwork? Bird-like footprints? Or maybe an ancient language?

Parker's finger throbbed and ached until she pointed it at the screen. The markings were transcribed into English. Parker quickly began reading out loud.

Stefanos, My Son,

Somewhere beneath the sky and the sea, my essence must go to rest among the rushing waters and the towers of branches that make up our world. My time has come to join our Forefathers, the Ruling Great Ones, our Sky Kings who guide our wise owls, the Spirits of the Sky. One is never ready. But we are only visitors on this planet. Now, I must leave the rule of our wondrous Spyridon to you.

I know your time has come before you have prepared. My time arrived earlier than I had planned. We can never predict our time nor know the precise moment the Spirits decide is best for us to rule. When we are called, we must be ready.

I warn you as my father warned me, and his father warned him. Before the Spirits call, it will not be pleasant, and you will lose yourself, as the Spirits' cries grow louder. All your guidance, all of your good work, must take place before your hundredth birthday. Your course must be in place, or it will be too late for you to control your powers.

Though you may think it is not your time to lead, you will be a wiser and better leader than I. You are a true Ruler, a

Great One with patience and foresight, qualities that will ensure a bright and better future for Spyridon.

You know to keep those out of favor close to your heart. They need to stay under your watchful eye. Your loyalists will not wrong you. And your earthlings must be protected. You must teach them our ways before it is too late. They will be the emissaries of the future—the future of both Spyridon and Earth long after you are gone. Those who choose to stay will take on the serum of our blood.

A hot and stinging shock physically jolted Parker.

"Belliza—the serum of blood! What does that mean?" She searched Belliza's eyes for an explanation. "I don't understand."

Belliza turned away and soared into the air. From the height of the Sky Box, Belliza stared down at Parker for an instant and blinked her eyes.

Parker could barely speak. Perspiration soaked her body. She stared into the clouds searching for Belliza. Dizzy and light-headed, Parker sank into herself and collapsed on the floor. She choked and tried to catch her breath, feeling as if she was smothered.

Outside the Sky Box, a burst of fire shot from the clouds, directly toward them. Another fiery cloud exploded. The floor inside swayed and the room went black.

Parker called out into the darkness. Her feet and hands went stone cold. Pins and needles riddled her arms and legs. Her body shivered and her heart pulsed frantically.

She couldn't think clearly or process what had transpired. She stretched her arms out, searching for Edison and Henley. "Where are you? Henley? Edison?"

"We're both here, Parker! Over here!" Edison said.

Parker finally exhaled. "Thank God! Keep talking and stretch out your hands to me!"

"We're over here. Over here!" Parker inched her body along the dark floor, moving closer to their voices. Finally, she touched their hands and huddled into them.

Had the attack escalated? Had it spread to the Citadel? Had the Upperworld not been able to contain the battle on Katamoor?

Suddenly, small, prickly bird feet landed on top of her head. Two beams of light illuminated from above. At the opposite end of the room, rooted in the midst of the sphere of radiance, Cole walked toward her.

Disheveled, his hair wild and his face grave, he barely resembled himself.

"Cole! Are we being attacked again at the Citadel?"

Belliza fluttered away from Parker's head and rose to the top of the Sky Box. She showered more light from her eyes and flooded the Sky Box in bright white.

Cole's eyes dwelled on Parker and shifted to Henley and Edison.

"Are you guys okay?"

"We're okay. I think." Parker said as she eyed her companions. "But what is going on?"

"The Citadel took a big hit. Far worse than the attack on the night you arrived. The Virago Trees are practically destroyed and Katamoor is in danger of sinking into the sea. There have been simultaneous blasts in key outposts across every region." He stopped speaking. "But I came here first to check on you. I am grateful you all made it to the Sky Box. I fear we have lost many lives again. Whoever is behind the attacks is out to destroy us. You are safe here. Just stay put. I'll be back. This time don't move! Any of you. Belliza, stay with them until I return. Don't let them out of your sight."

"Where are you going?" Parker asked.

"I told you. I am going to fix this. I confronted Stefanos. He will be at peace with what must be done. Now I am going to deal with the Empress. You made me realize I have to step up. I cannot allow this to continue. The Empress will listen. Or I will do what I have to do." He crossed the room and leaned into Parker, quickly stealing a quick kiss from her lips.

"Please don't go!" Parker begged.

Her words fell in the empty space. Cole had vanished within seconds.

Unsteady, Parker quickly rose to her feet. Blood rushed to her head and she swooned. The enormity of the devastation of all they had created and all they had worked toward was too huge to grasp. She wiped her sweaty palms on her sheath and stared at Belliza.

"Belliza, where is the Silver Helm?"

Henley and Edison glared at her. "Are you crazy?" Edison yelled. "You can't be serious. You are not going to the Underworld, Parker."

"Oh yes I am!"

Henley motioned to Belliza to come closer. "You can't let her go, Belliza. Stop her! You heard what Cole said!"

The bird tipped her beak, waving Parker on, to follow Cole.

Henley crossed her arms. "This has gotten out of control. If you go, we're not coming after you, Parker. You're on your own. They have all the power and knowledge down there. It's way too dangerous."

"I'm with her," Edison added. "Parker, you are putting your life at risk down there. Do you want to die? For him?"

"I'm not going to die. I am going to live and make sure we all live." She turned back to Belliza. "Where is the Silver Helm? I am going with it or without it."

Belliza circled the far glass wall and Parker read her mind, 'this is the wall that will lead you to the Silver Helm.' Parker leveled her index finger at the glass. A stinging pulse of energy surged down her arm and into her hand. She fell off her feet with the force of the current. The bird nodded, confirming silently, 'Take this path.'

With her head high, she raced from the Sky Box and into the dusty, smoke-laden corridor of the Citadel. A pocket of smog condensed before her eyes and revealed a hidden cubicle. The electric force stung her again and prodded her toward the cubicle. Water streamed down her neck and along her back, soaking her tunic like a second skin. Her hair plastered her head. She spun in search of Belliza. "What kind of crazy thing is this, Belliza? Are these cubbies everywhere?"

Belliza had disappeared. Parker stepped into the cubicle. The wall closed and the familiar prickling of the Silver Helm attacked her body. She focused on the path ahead that would take her through the branches in the Citadel's foundation. From there, she planned to backtrack by way of the Black Sea to the Grotto.

She moved through the dense smog barely able to make her way along the corridors. Choking, she breathed in a foul chemical odor and smoke threatened to fill her lungs and chest. She pressed her arm against her face, covering her nostrils, and hurried on. The further she walked, the denser the air became, and the higher the temperature rose. In the distance, caws and shrieks moaned in mourning.

Stretching to move through the top branches, she thrust her arms from limb to limb, until she finally reached the base, the entry to the cloudscape, and the last path to the South Gate. Exhausted, Parker prayed the cushion of the cloudy walk before her would ease the difficulty of her movement. Her legs, sore and bruised, jostled with every jump and ached as her muscles absorbed the shock. Her eyes remained focused beneath her. She was determined not to miss the well-hidden passage buried between the cloud formations.

After a few miles, she dropped to her knees and began crawling, hoping the worst of the air quality would rise above her. She groped past fragments of bones, smelled burnt flesh, feathers, and clothing. She blocked out thoughts of the remains, and their origin. She would crawl all the way, if she must, even though her hands and knees blistered and bled.

The electricity within her didn't ease. The currents jerked her movements over and over again striking her as if she were a Pavlovian dog prodded to follow direction.

chapter thirty-four

Parker had traveled a good distance. If she remembered the path correctly, she should be near the portal. She peered over her shoulder one last time to view the Citadel, now far in the distance. Her body vibrated and her ears rang with the unpleasant hum of her adrenaline pumping like a fever eating up her insides. But mostly the sense of being alone in the midst of the horror was beginning to erode her earlier bravado.

She spotted a camouflaged fossil wrapped with feathers and twigs—the traveler's warning she'd recognized from the Labyrinth. She touched the rock for good luck and silently thanked the traveler who had marked the way. The path narrowed quickly, and descended, becoming a tight and dank tunnel. Her mouth went dry and she swallowed hard to retrieve saliva. She bit her cheeks and called up her courage.

At the curve up ahead, she noticed another traveler's stone marking the end of the tunnel. She had entered the first layer of the Underworld, still dark and murky. She had ventured into the Labyrinth that led to the Black Sea.

Breathless and thirsty, she kept to the path, the same one she followed with Cole and returned them to safety, but now in reverse. The waters of the Black Sea slapped up against the boulders lining its shores. The sound was close by. The light diminished and the air moistened with each step. She shuddered, wanting to forget the darkness and the mystery of the Underworld she had re-entered. She shoved away her fear of the strange sea creatures, the unnatural flowing movements, and her bizarre ability to breathe beneath the sea without an oxygen source.

Parker distinguished voices. Cole's voice, and then someone else. It couldn't have been the tongue-less Veto. A snapping, curling sound startled her, and she practically jumped out of her skin. The unmistakable voice of the Scavenger's laugh reverberated through the tunnels. Nearing the black abyss that fell away into forever, she moved stealthily through the passage for a closer view. She hid behind a group of large boulders, still cautious though the Silver Helm protected her.

The scene before her caused her to gasp despite herself.

Up ahead, Cole, bound at the hands and feet, suspended from a rope, dangled over the waters of the Black Sea. A guard with a huge snake head and elongated dorsal fins stood beside Veto. The guard wore the uniform of the Underworld and held a barbed whip. He cracked the spiraling lash on Cole's back. Scavenger scuttled around the guard, watching and smirking as each stripe appeared on Cole's back.

The blood dripped from Cole's body and trickled into the water, tantalizing several electric eels swirling through the black waters beneath him. Their eerie grins signaled their thirst for a bite of flesh, though Cole was just out of reach.

"They're licking their choppers for you, Sky Man. They like a ration of bird seed now and then. I'd say you've gotten yourself into a fine mess, Lieutenant," Scavenger called out. "You helped the earthling escape and you'll pay the price."

"Let me go. I am warning you. I will have your head if you don't release me."

"If I were a betting man, I would wager you have no way to negotiate your freedom this time around. Your pool of influence with the Empress is poisoned. Fool the Empress but once. Now you are the fool, Sky Man, for returning to the Underworld."

Parker stared at Cole about to scream when she saw the silver eels circling beneath him. The creatures snapped their jagged teeth and swam impatiently, waiting their turn, lured by each drop of Cole's blood.

Two more uniformed soldiers stood off to the water's edge laughing. Both wore blades on their belts and carried swords. The Scavenger wore blades on each of his eight legs and twirled a sword in each hand. A crossbow with a pack of arrows slung over his shell. The large guard with the snake head continued curling the lash to the Scavenger's orders, striking Cole without interruption.

Parker worried she hadn't brought any weapons. How

was she going to put an end to this?

"The Sky Man flies low tonight," a guard without the lash chuckled. The other pranced about the boulders and flapped his arms like wings. The two joked heartily and walked right by Parker continuing their antics, less than a foot away.

The Scavenger called out to them, "Settle down, you two. Branson, you and Gibeon return to the Grotto and let the sentries know we'll be on our way shortly. I want the gallows prepped for this fool. The Empress announced anyone who desires may shoot an arrow into his heart. Not that it will be beating," he cackled. "Now—off with you. Veto and I will bring him back."

She couldn't let the torture continue. How much could Cole take? What if he passed out? They'd drop him into the water. Her heart pounded in her chest and the tears flowed down her cheeks. She had to stop crying and do something.

She took a deep breath and pulled herself together.

She aimed her finger at the Scavenger, but a noise startled her from behind. A massive, dark feathered creature lumbered toward her and edged near the waters of the Black Sea. Parker shook her head in disbelief as she made out the enormous figure of an Upperworlder not wearing the Silver Helm. But who could be walking the trail? A limited few knew the location of the access portal at the East Gate. The body came closer and Parker fell to her knees.

Vibius! He had paused beside the Scavenger to observe Cole's torture.

"I had my suspicions you were part of this, Vibius," Cole said, exhausted, choking out the words with little breath. A deep, tortured breath later, he found his voice again. "But I didn't want to believe even you could be capable of this." Weak, his voice low, almost inaudible, he said, "You have shown me what you are. A traitor! You've betrayed our Sky King. And, all of us of the Upperworld."

"I'd watch your mouth, if I were you," Vibius said. "You have played both sides of our world. Neither of which belong to you. You are the last person on Spyridon who should call me a traitor."

"I tried to save this planet. Not destroy it like you, but to keep peace. You'll never be me. You don't have an honorable bone in your body, or you wouldn't be here. And you wouldn't be doing this!"

The guard with the snake head hissed and cracked the whip against Cole's leg, splitting open his pants. The blood pooled into the sea and the eels leapt out of the water, impatient for the promise of a meal.

"Sssssshall I finisssssh him off and drop him in, Captain?" The guard with the snake head asked the Scavenger.

"Not yet, Snakehead. The Empress has plans for this one. You can leave now. Catch up with Branson and Gibeon," Scavenger said.

"There is still time to save yourself, Vibius. It is time for the truth," Cole said. "You don't have to do this. Vibius, it was you all along!" Cole said, "You poisoned the waters of the Upperworld. And orchestrated the attacks!"

Parker sprang into action and landed on top of the largest boulder. Her foot slid against several loose pebbles, tossing them up into the air, then splashing into the Black Sea, and back onto Parker's legs. Veto and Scavenger spun around. At once, Vibius spotted Parker's legs on the shoreline, free of the Helm.

Parker raised her hand and willed the fire to come again. She only had one chance at this. A burst of heat streamed out of her hand, but Vibius moved and missed the fire. Of course, he'd seen it coming; he was an old war veteran and had the soldier's instincts Parker lacked. Her fire flashed against the cave wall where Vibius had been, and splattered Scavenger and Veto with hot shrapnel. The armless Veto opened his mouth in pain, but it was a pitiful, soundless attempt. He shuffled back behind the boulders, shielding himself from the stream of fiery blaze.

Scavenger rushed to help Vibius who had grabbed a rope from his belt. He unfurled the twine and lassoed Parker's ankle, pulling her leg from under her. She tumbled and fell against the boulder. She neither heard nor felt the crack of her head against the rock until she was on the ground. Her eyes glazed over.

"What a pity! Your timing is a bit off, earthling! Or maybe, your timing is just right. Now you can join our imposter. The Empress will be delighted to display the two of you for the price of one."

The old hawk motioned to Scavenger, "You can return to the Meridian. Sky Man's blood belongs to my hand. I'll have some of my own fun while I wait here with Veto for the sentries to help us lug the two bodies back." The Scavenger retreated, following the path the guards had taken.

Vibius tugged the rope on Parker's ankle and dragged her limp body to the edge of the water. Her head bounced against the loose gravel of the rocky path. Veto came closer. With one of the blades he wore on his leg, he kicked and punctured her ankles while Vibius bound both of Parker's legs together with rope.

Her eyes flashed open. She screamed as Vibius dug his free claw into her cheek with his talon. The pain roared across her skin and the blood flowed from her face. She stared at his talons, now smeared with her blood. He fidgeted with something around his neck and smiled. Parker squinted to better eye what he held in his bloodied claw. Vibius twirled the leather braid of the medallion that belonged to Stefanos!

"What a fool the Ruling Great One is to think you were smart enough, or strong enough to help the Upperworld." Vibius sputtered his words as he held the medallion.

"Let the girl be. This is between you and me." Cole said. "She has nothing to do with us."

"She wouldn't have lived for long anyway. Better to put an end to her now." Vibius said, then ordered, "Go join the guards, Veto. You should be able to improve your rank now with this capture. And make sure they've completed the work on the second display to showcase the earthling. We'll string her up next to her friend. I want the eels to have some fun with her, too. You'll be rewarded for this."

Veto didn't move. Vibius craned his neck and ordered, "Go on with you. And come back with some more help. I'm not touching this filth. Either one of them. There's nothing they can do now."

Vibius waited until Veto disappeared down the trail. He edged toward the shoreline and said, "Now, where were we, Cole?"

"You killed Pantione and the children, too. Didn't you? I've held on to the poison samples from the water. It's the same poison used to murder the royal family," Cole said. "I presume the Empress doesn't know."

Vibius laughed and stroked his feathered neck. "Ah yes. Well, you're almost correct. But unfortunately, Pantione isn't dead. He carries a vial of protective serum with him at all times. It saved him from the poison. He's in a coma and expected to live."

Riveted by the news, perspiring, Parker's thoughts raced. Pantione was alive! Vibius the murderer of the children! What kind of monster was he? And she could have been killed for his crimes!

She moved her hands to touch her legs. They were completely numb. She couldn't feel anything! The blood oozed down the left side of her shredded face. Her arms and hands tingled and throbbed.

"The Empress knew he had the serum," Vibius said. "But she wasn't sure he would make it. Foiled my plans a bit. But I'll get to him. After I finish you off. I'll take care of the other earthlings too, and then the Empress. Stefanos is already on his way out. I am destined to rule Spyridon."

Parker heard enough. Her fingers twitched and electric currents of energy surged to the tips. She targeted Vibius' eyes and unleashed a flare of fire at him. He screamed. His feathers burned and his eyes smoldered. He flew into the air and dove into the water, emerging immediately from the Black Sea, his eyes unseeing and ruined.

"Speak now or I will kill you instantly. My eyes may be blinded, Parker. But I know your scent," Vibius said. "You can't hide from me. I will track you wherever you go. You think you have powers because you can shoot fire from your fingers. You will never be one of us! You will never rule the Upperworld. I will make certain of that."

Parker remained quiet and untied her legs, gathering the bloody rope to free Cole. She pulled Cole into her arms and the weight of his body dropped on top of her and they rolled onto a bed of sand and moss, Parker flung on top of him. In spite of her pain, his warmth spread through her again, sending a renewed source of strength. She untied his hands and feet and her body poured into his. She covered his lips with her mouth. The blood on her face merged with his sweat.

Vibius swooped down to Parker, grabbed her hair in his talons, and pulled her up into the air. As Vibius ascended, Cole yanked the blade from Vibius' ankle strap and sliced the giant hawk, clipping off one of his wings. Vibius lost his balance. His injured wing weakened, he dropped Parker to the ground. Cole circled his rope around Vibius, pulling it tightly so the hawk couldn't move.

Veto reappeared from behind the boulders and thrust

two of his blades into Parker's leg with a kick from his foot.

She held Cole's gaze. His thoughts were written on his face: the concern for her safety, the knowledge that she had the power to undo Veto with a thought.

Veto quivered, and must have guessed what was about to happen, because his blade sent a quick flash. He sliced Parker again with his foot, this time a shallower cut, because he was already halfway down the passage, running away. She tried to call up the fire, but between the shock of being slashed again, the pain of it, and Veto's cowardice, she couldn't make it in time. The fire bashed into the cavern wall just as the armless guard disappeared around a large boulder.

Cole let out a shaky breath. *Close call,* his thoughts told her. Then he turned his attention back to the betrayer.

"Now, it's time for a little chat, Vibius," Cole said. "Admit it to me. Tell me, was it your idea to attack the Upperworld when the earthlings arrived? Tell me, you poisoned our waters and the Underworld royals. We wondered if it could have been an Upperworlder behind this. But only Upperworld royals and earthlings can survive here. We never considered a royal would do this." Vibius spit in Cole's direction.

"You'll talk. Or say goodbye to your other wing." Cole demanded.

"I have nothing to say to you. Go ahead, take it off."

Parker watched Cole in horror. "Stop, Cole. He's wearing Stefanos' medallion. Stefanos would never give it to him."

Communicating telepathically with Cole, Parker sent a message she was worried about Stefanos. *We have to return to the Upperworld and make sure the Sky King is not in danger,* Parker told him.

The jovial voices of the returning guards echoed down the tunnels from far off. Parker let out a deep breath and silently communicated, *Please, let's leave the Black Sea and return to the tunnel back to the Upperworld. They're coming back! We can't fight off all of them.*

"Not yet." Cole said. "Lose your other wing, Vibius, or tell me did you plan the attacks on the Upperworld? The destruction of the mangrove? Was it you?"

"I owe you nothing, Cole. You'll get no answers from me. I was the better leader. Better than Stefanos. And certainly, far better than Parker who will never be what I could have been. Let her take on the Empress now."

Cole picked up Vibius' bloodied sword and thrust it into the hawk's heart as he lifted the bronze medallion from around Vibius' neck.

"He didn't deserve an easy death," Cole said.

"We both could have died, Cole. I've never felt fear like that. Fear for you. And fear for me."

He pulled her toward him and kissed her, this time harder. She felt the desperate need in his kiss and responded by kissing him deeper. Cole's fingers fluttered over the skin on her cheeks, hardly daring to touch her, what with the blood still seeping out. He tore the hem of his vest and wrapped it tightly around her head, to try to control the bleeding.

"That'll have to do for now. We have a way to go until we reach the tunnel. Guess we'll be leaving a nice bloody trail for them to follow."

They limped over the boulders, putting distance between them and the Black Sea.

"The Underworlders won't follow us inside the tunnel though," Cole said. "This close to the Upperworld means the Spirits of the Sky can aid us. The Underworlders fear them. We'll be safe —we just have to make it there."

The voices were closer now. From behind, she thought she heard footsteps and voices, but her imagination was working overtime. They disappeared silently into the darkness of the entry to the portal.

chapter thirty-five

P arker and Cole entered the Roost to find Belliza
hovering beside Stefanos. The Ruling Great One
lay on his back, propped up by cushions. The ever-
bright room, now desolate, was cloaked in darkness. As
they approached, Belliza surprised Parker with the sound
of her voice. "We've been waiting for you, Parker. I am glad
you are here." Belliza motioned to Parker, "Come zit
bezide our Zky King. I will leave you now. He wantz to
zpeak with you." She flew into the cloudy corridor and as
she was about to vanish, she said, "Cole, Ztefanoz azked
that you ztay with Parker. You are to be his witnezz."

Covered in head-to-toe white dust and barely stirring,
Stefanos whispered to Parker, "I knew my time was
coming, though I am not ready. But I must be. Come
closer," he faintly whispered.

Parker knelt beside him.

"You are the One."

Parker gave him a blank stare, tears blurring her vision.
"What are you saying, Stefanos?" Parker asked, her voice

unsteady, her worry rising as she wrestled with fear.

"You will be my successor. You are the One. The next Ruling Great One, Parker. The Sky Queen. The One if by land. The One who has come to us by way of Earth. As my father, Zonoros, planned."

"But…" she stammered. "I thought it would be my choice—my choice to return to Earth. My choice to go home."

His chest rose and fell slowly. Tears formed in Parker's eyes as she turned away.

"The choice will always be with you, just as it was from the beginning." He stopped and gathered his thoughts. "I wanted to die quickly and join the Spirits of the Sky. Our wise owls know war must come and then it will pass. Just the same as we leaders must know, Parker. I am not afraid. You must not be afraid either."

Parker stroked his brow. "You can't leave us yet. Spyridon needs you. Your wisdom." Her words lingered. Then she said, "I need you, Stefanos."

"My calling is no longer here, Parker. Not of this world. But the next one. I will watch over you from afar. You will feel me from above the clouds and hear my voice in the whistle of the Spirits. The wise owls. You know what you must do. It is your turn now." His knotty talons spread and clasped her hand. "Cole will be here for you. You can trust him. Listen to his truth. He knows the way of our world."

Stefanos' eyes flickered. "Cole, promise me you will help Parker stay the course."

"Yes, Sky King. You know I will."

Stefanos closed his eyes and his chest rose and fell slowly. He barely moved.

Parker collapsed into Cole's arms. He caressed her head, stroked her hair, and held her tightly in his arms.

She cried uncontrollably. Sobs racked her body. She wanted to be comforted. She wanted the touch of Cole's lips. She peered into his eyes. "How is anything ever going to be right again? I don't understand any of this. We read a letter in the Sky Box. That I…that we, Henley, Edison, and me, we have the blood of Spyridon? But—we are supposed to go home."

As Cole started to reply, the Roost filled with light. The air cleared. Cole's hands dropped. "It's a sign, Parker," Cole said. "Stefanos has passed. But you know now he will be watching over you." He reached out his hand and held her tightly.

She pulled her hand away. She needed to think. She walked over to the glass wall. She searched for the Virago Trees, feeling desperate and lost on a planet on which she didn't belong, but had come to understand. A chill passed through her. She wrapped her arms around herself. Absentmindedly, she rubbed her upper arms. But something caught her attention, something felt strange. Her skin. The texture was different. Fuzzy. Confused, she raised her forearm and looked closely.

There on her arm, the skin glistened with the tiniest layer of feathers like clusters of gold.

acknowledgements

I wonder how many authors would admit their first novel would have been doomed to rest in peace had they known the arduous path leading to publication. Being both blessed and cursed to believe in myself and follow my dreams, I had no option but to finish what I had begun.

I owe my perseverance to my parents and grandparents who enriched my life with their values and taught me there are no limits to what you can accomplish. I believed you.

To my brother, Stephen, from the eyes of heaven, I hope you recognize your integrity and profound wisdom in my lead character, your namesake.

To my loving husband, Michael, although you did gently inquire about my progress, your supremely generous nature and belief in my talent provided me with the opportunity and the space to finish *One If.*

To my sons, Jeffrey and David, you are the epitome of the best of my characters—and you know exactly which ones I mean.

To Judi, Courtney, and Jaime— you are my women and the wind beneath my wings. And in this case, wings were part of the plan!

Professionally, to my forever colleague, Lou, I curse you and thank you simultaneously for planting the seed for this book no matter how I kicked and screamed down the path.

To my editors and professional associates—Teresa, Katrina, Paula, Brent, and the Pound Ridge Author Society, specifically, Nancy and Paula—without your support this book wouldn't have come to fruition.

Equally important, I thank my first readers for their honest feedback. Theresa, Shiv, Sammi, Lisa, Emma, you were my green light, and then some.

About the Author

Carol B. Allen is an author and international, award-winning creative professional. She has held leadership positions in firms that believe in strengthening community across the New York Tri State Area. She plays an active role in supporting opportunities to enhance young women's interest in the STEM fields as well as advancing causes that protect the environment.

She serves on the Advisory Board for Advancing Women in Science and Medicine (AWSM), part of Northwell Health's Feinstein Institute for Medical Research. Additionally, she has participated on the Advisory Committee for the Girl Scouts STEM program.

A University of Michigan graduate, Carol received high honors and the prestigious Student of Distinction recognition.

Carol resides in Westchester County and is an active member of the Pound Ridge Authors Society. When she isn't writing, Carol enjoys the city life and the country life, balancing her time with her family, exploring the cultural offerings of Manhattan as well as the great outdoors of the bucolic Northeast woodlands.

A Note from the Author...
I realize that *One If* poses many questions and my readers want to know more. Please feel free to drop me a note at www.carolballen.com.

CPSIA information can be obtained
at www.ICGtesting.com
Printed in the USA
BVHW070451211221
624510BV00014B/717

9 781734 342406